Campus Tramp

LAWRENCE BLOCK
writing as Andrew Shaw

CAMPUS TRAMP

LAWRENCE BLOCK writing as ANDREW SHAW

Copyright © 1959 Lawrence Block

All Rights Reserved.

This is a work of fiction. Names, characters, places, and incidents are the products of the author's imagination or are used fictitiously. Any resemblance to actual events, locales, or persons is entirely coincidental.

Cover and Interior Design by QA Productions

A LAWRENCE BLOCK PRODUCTION

Classic Erotica

21 Gay Street
Candy
Gigolo Johnny Wells
April North
Carla
A Strange Kind of Love
Campus Tramp
Community of Women
Born to be Bad
College for Sinners
Of Shame and Joy
A Woman Must Love
The Adulterers
The Twisted Ones
High School Sex Club
I Sell Love
69 Barrow Street
Four Lives at the Crossroads
Circle of Sinners
A Girl Called Honey
Sin Hellcat
So Willing

Classic Erotica #7

Campus Tramp

Lawrence Block

Chapter 1

The girl had soft honey-blond hair that she wore in a long pony tail. Her pale green sweater hugged breasts that were alive with youth and full with a maturity that didn't go with the little-girl face or the virginal innocence in her hazel eyes. The skirt that was tight on rounded hips and muscular thighs was a Black Watch plaid, with dark greens and blues predominating.

The girl was sitting on a train. The seat next to hers was unoccupied, and she was sprawled out so that she managed to take up both of the seats. Her head was close to the window, and if her eyes had been open she would have been able to look out on fields where corn had been recently harvested, fields where a few sheep or cows wandered peacefully. But the girl was deep in thought and her eyes were closed.

The girl's name was Linda Shepard. The train's name was the Ohio State Limited, a New York Central passenger train that went from New York to Cincinnati via Albany, Syracuse, Rochester, Buffalo, Cleveland, Columbus, Springfield and Dayton. The girl had boarded the train in Cleveland and she would leave it in Springfield to catch a Greyhound bus to Clifton.

There was, as far as she knew, only one reason in the world for a person to go to Clifton, Ohio. The town was the home of three thousand people who were born, went to school, worked, married, and finally died in Clifton. Some of them managed to get away from the town at some stage in their development, and she was fairly confident that anybody who left Clifton would be careful never to return.

But Clifton was also the site of Clifton College, an institution of learning which managed to add another 1500 souls to Clifton's meager population. The college, which seemed to Linda to be the only point in Clifton's favor, was the reason for her presence on the Ohio State Limited.

She was excited. She was quite motionless in her seat and her eyes were closed, but she was excited nevertheless. She was about to enter Clifton College as a freshman, and she knew that she was going to enter a totally different world at the same time. Clifton was only a little over 200 miles from Cleveland, but it was going to be much farther away as far as she was concerned.

Linda was eighteen. Except for summers at camp and the class trip to Washington during Easter vacation of her senior year, she had spent all of those eighteen years in Cleveland, living with her mother and father in a moderate-sized brick house in Shaker Heights. When she went out on dates she went with boys she knew from school, generally boys she had known for most of her life. When she did things they were the things everybody else did. Her life in Cleveland was by no means dull, but the feeling persisted that it wasn't entirely *her* life—she had no responsibility for herself, no choice in what she did or what role she played.

But college would be different. Not the academic part of it, not that. To tell the truth, she thought, she didn't much care about books or classes. If all she had wanted was an education she could have done much better in her own home town at Western

Reserve. No, education in the classroom was important, but there were other things that were a good deal more important.

Growing up.

Thinking.

Maturing.

Learning to be a woman.

She stretched in her seat and glanced out of the window. *Learning to be a woman.* She wondered what it was that would change a girl to a woman. Age? She was eighteen now, and that left her somewhere in the middle between Girl and Woman. She was old enough to marry but not old enough to vote. Old enough to drink hard liquor in New York but too young to drink anything stronger than 3.2 beer in Ohio.

Old enough, under the law, to let a man make love to her.

She closed her eyes again and a smile bloomed on her face, a gentle and secret smile, as if she knew something that nobody else in the entire world knew. *Old enough to make love,* she thought to herself, and she thought about making love and what it was and when it was wrong and when it was right and what a wild, strange, wonderful mystery it was.

Linda Shepard was a virgin.

This was hardly extraordinary. Howard and Norma Shepard would have been quite justifiably surprised and annoyed if their daughter hadn't managed to get through Corry Senior High School with her maidenhead intact, and Linda herself took it for granted that she would graduate from high school with her virginity unimpaired. Nice girls from Shaker Heights simply didn't have sexual intercourse during high school. It was as simple as that, and there had never been an occasion when it seemed either desirable or proper for Linda to change her status.

Well, she reflected, that wasn't altogether true. There was a time when she came much closer to sex than she had expected—a rather pleasant time, all things considered. She had been dating Chuck Connor steadily, going out with him two or three times a week and seeing him in school almost every day. They went to movies and parties and dances, and they spent more and more time parked on a quiet lane in the blue Pontiac that Chuck borrowed from his father.

More time and more time.

They were both seniors. Chuck was taller than she was, a rangy boy with sandy hair and freckles on his face. He was a good athlete—captain of the basketball team that year and a major letter man in track. You couldn't call him handsome, but he was extremely attractive and quite sure of himself socially.

He kissed her goodnight after their first date. Their goodnight kisses took longer as time went by, and it wasn't long before they were kissing in the car in front of her house instead of on her front porch. And she enjoyed the kissing, with Chuck's strong arms gentle around her and his mouth pressed to hers.

From the porch to the car. From in front of the house to a lane where no houses had been built and where passing cars were few and far between. From kissing to necking, from necking to heavier petting.

You had to stop somewhere. You were the girl, so you had to call the shots and tell Chuck when to stop, had to insist upon it and make sure he let go of you and put his hands on the wheel and turned his key in the ignition and drove you home. He expected it. He wanted it that way, because that was the way the pattern demanded it. That was the standard routine, with the boy going as far as he could and the girl making sure that he didn't go too far.

The boy couldn't stop of his own accord. If he did he lost face and seemed less a man for it, although Linda would have been willing to bet that there were times Chuck would have preferred to stop before they both got so excited that stopping was an effort and a frustration. But that was the pattern, and when you lived in Shaker Heights and went to Corry Senior High School you played things by the book and stuck close to the pattern.

It was a tough pattern to stick to. The people who figured out the pattern evidently didn't take into consideration the fact that sometimes you didn't want to stop, sometimes you were a girl who felt like a woman and who wanted to be treated like a woman and loved like a woman. But it was easier to keep the pattern than to break it.

Most of the time.

But one time was different from the others. She remembered it very clearly—it was the night of the senior prom, with exams coming up in a week or so and graduation only a few weeks in the future. They went to the prom together and danced almost every dance, and then she and Chuck went off with Sue Lewis and Jack Morgan and drank rye whiskey from a flask that Jack carried in the glove compartment of his car. She had never had straight liquor before—her drinking had been limited to a very occasional highball before dinner with her parents. The rye burned its way down her throat, but after the second gulp from the flask she didn't mind the hot sensation in her throat any more. It was pleasant—warm and relaxing and buoyant.

She didn't get drunk, just a little bit high. And then Sue and Jack went off in Jack's car and she and Chuck were alone. Chuck's hand found hers and led her to their car and they drove off into the night without saying a word. She sat close to him and rested her head on his shoulder, and he slipped one arm around her and guided the car easily with his left hand.

Their usual parking place was empty, the rest of the lane deserted. Chuck eased the Pontiac off the road and turned off the ignition. Then he doused the lights.

He turned to her.

She remembered it clearly, very clearly, every detail fresh and sharp in her mind. Her eyes were closed now and she went over what followed in her mind, picturing it and feeling it and living it again . . .

His arms went around her and her mouth came up to meet his. His lips were gentle at first, very gentle, and she liked the way the musky odor of his sweat mixed and mingled with his after-shave lotion. His lips bore down upon hers and her mouth opened. His tongue snuck between her lips, running over her lips and teeth, touching her tongue.

The kiss took a long time to end. Then he released her and looked deep into her eyes, his own eyes boring into hers. She knew what was on his mind—there could be only one thing, and it was a thing neither of them wanted to talk about. There was so little time, hardly any time at all before he would be off to work at a Canadian camp for the summer while she remained in the city. Then she would go to Clifton while he went east to M.I.T. Very little time, just a few weeks.

For a year now they had belonged to each other. For a year

they had spent all their free time together, getting to know each other, starting to fall in love.

So little time left.

"Linda," he said. That was all, just her name, but there was a huskiness in his voice that said all the things he couldn't say.

He kissed her again. She pulled him close to her so that her breasts were warm and tight against his chest and this time it was her tongue that probed deep into his mouth, her tongue that sought his and sent little shivers of desire through both of them.

And this kiss lasted longer than the one before it. When they forced themselves apart they exchanged another deep, searching look and she could read his thoughts in his eyes. He wanted her, wanted her very much, wanted more than the kissing and touching and loving-by-inches that she had permitted him so far.

She wanted it, too.

When he kissed her a third time his hand found her breast and held it tenderly like a little boy holding a baby bird. She was wearing a frilly formal and she wished silently that she was wearing something else because the frills were too much of a barrier between her breast and his hand. She wished that she was wearing nothing, nothing at all, so that his hands could hold her and stroke her and love her and make her feel like a woman.

"Linda."

She looked at him.

"Honey, let's get into the back seat."

There were beads of sweat standing out on his forehead and she wondered if she was perspiring with desire herself. She looked at him, hungry but frightened.

"Why?"

"It's roomier back there."

"There's enough room up front."

He took a deep breath. Then he said: "Damn steering wheel keeps getting in my way. Come on, honey—let's get in the back."

Why not? she thought. She nodded silently and he smiled. He got out of the car and walked around to open the door for her. It made her smile, the way he was such a gentleman even at a time like this, opening doors for her when both of them were so hot for each other they could have just as easily hopped over the seat to save time.

She got out of the car and let him open the back door for her. She climbed inside and he followed her and took her in his arms, his mouth clamping down on hers. She felt the blood rushing through her veins and she ached for him to kiss her, to touch her, to take her and possess her completely.

As he went to kiss her again he tried to get his hand into the front of her dress. The dress was cut low enough so that the cleft between her two full breasts was barely visible, but it was tight on her body and he was forced to reach for her breast awkwardly.

She pushed him away, whispering: "I'll take care of it." Then her hands reached behind her back and played with first the hook-and-eye attachment and then the zipper. Then she shrugged her shoulders and the dress fell away from her to the waist.

She went into his arms and his hand fastened on her breast. She could feel his fingers through the lacy black bra as he kneaded the firm flesh lovingly. She began to breathe faster and he kissed her again, his fingers still gentle but more insistent.

She pushed him away and he stared at her. Then she flashed him a smile and she could see the tension go out of his face.

"Let me get rid of this," she said. Her hands went around her back once more and a second later the bra was off, unneeded and abandoned on the floor of the car. She looked up at him and saw the emotion shining in his eyes, equal parts of awe and desire and admiration.

He reached out one hand hesitantly and the tips of his fingers brushed the nipple of her breast. A shiver went through her but she remained motionless, pulse racing, breathing deeply.

He had never seen her like this before, she knew. In the past she had felt the thrill of his hands on her bare breasts but never before had she stripped to the waist for him to look upon and touch her. Before she used to undo her bra so that he could reach up under her sweater and hold her, but this was different, somehow bolder and far more exciting.

"Linda," he said. His voice was hoarse.

She didn't say anything. She didn't have to.

"You're beautiful," he said. "I can barely believe how beautiful you are."

Sitting there so close to him with his eyes warm on her breasts she knew she was beautiful. She felt beautiful, beautiful with her skin smooth and cool and white, beautiful with her breasts bare and firm and pink at the nipples.

She said: "Touch me, Chuck."

He pulled her around and forced her down so that she lay on her back across him with her head cradled in the crook of his right arm. He cupped both her breasts with his hands and held them, squeezing them gently, and she felt her nipples growing taut and firm under his touch. His mouth found hers and he kissed her. Then he bent over her and kissed her breasts, first one and then the other, and she thought she would burst from the pure sensual excitement that was coursing through her young body.

When they broke apart this time neither of them was able to breathe easily. This was unlike anything they had ever experienced before. This wasn't kid stuff, high school kissing games in a parked car on a lonely road. They were caught up instead in something new and different, something hot and exciting, and they didn't know what to do about it. Love didn't enter into it at all—it was passion, sheer physical passion, and it was changing them from children to adults.

He kept kissing her, kept touching and kissing and licking her breasts, kept exciting her until she thought she was going to go out of her mind with the need for him. Then she felt his hand on her leg, on first her calf and then her knee. Her breathing became even heavier and she wanted to shout for him to stop. He had to stop, had to stop or in a moment she wouldn't be able to stop him. And it was getting dangerous now. It was getting far too close to something she didn't want to happen.

Or did she want it? Half of her wanted it. Her body wanted him, wanted him so much she could fairly scream for the want. But in her mind she was afraid, afraid and unready for what threatened to take place.

His hand was on her thigh. Her eyes had dropped shut but she opened them for a moment and saw the expression in his eyes. And she wondered if she would be able to stop him even if she wanted to.

His hand moved higher. His fingers were playing desperate little games with the skin on the inside of her thighs and she began to writhe involuntarily on the seat of the car, her body taking up the rhythms and movements of love easily, instinctively, like a baby automatically suckling on the nipple placed between his gums.

He moved away from her, his hands still working their subtle magic on her, and he was pushing her dress up over her thighs to her waist, baring the black panties that matched the bra. He tore his shirt open and flung himself down on top of her so that her breasts pressed into his bare chest. Her head was back and her eyelids were clenched shut. Without even thinking she reached her arms around him and crushed him to her, holding him and loving him, wanting him with a brand-new passion that seemed to grow more intense every second, needing him so much it was killing her.

Then he drew away from her once again. She couldn't even move while his fingers slipped under the elastic band of the flimsy panties and pulled them down over her hips, past her thighs and knees and calves and feet until they joined the matching bra on the floor.

When he touched her where she was itching to be touched a hot spasm of desire shot through her whole body and she moaned once, a whimpering little moan that only served to intensify his desire. His fingers continued to stroke her there and she churned under his touch, a thing of passion and virgin fire, a little girl who had turned into a woman who wanted her man.

She opened her eyes to see him fumbling with his own clothing, loosening his belt and lowering his pants and preparing to take her. She wanted to shout, to scream, and she even managed to open her mouth for a scream. But his fingers reached for her and touched her again where he had never touched before that night.

The scream died in her throat.

Her brain was shouting. Her brain was shrieking warning after warning to her but she let the warnings pass unheeded. She turned off her brain and listened only to her body.

He said: "Linda."

If he hadn't said anything, if he had just continued to do what he had started to do she would have been powerless to stop him and her virginity would have become a memory in the back seat of the blue Pontiac. But his voice murmuring her name came like a knife to slash her into awareness. In one motion she pushed him away and rolled over on her side, away from him.

"Linda! You can't stop now!"

But now she could stop. It was easy now for her to stop, very easy, and all his arguments wouldn't change her mind. Finally, at his request, she touched him the way he showed her to touch him and did the things with her hands that he wanted her to do while he lay with his hands on her thighs and his face buried in the gully between her breasts. She held him and touched him and squirmed under his touch until it happened for him and he lay all weak and limp and flaccid in her arms. She wished that his hands on her had brought her the relief that she had given him, but she was still tense and unfulfilled, restless and unsatisfied. She held him in her arms and gradually her own body ceased trembling. They lay in each other's arms for several minutes; then he sat up and they dressed and drove home in silence.

It was never the same again for them. She knew that if he had known more about sex, if he had known what to do, he would have taken her and possessed her without giving her the opportunity of refusing him. And he knew that he had done something wrong, something clumsy, and that her refusal was something which could have been avoided if he had known what he was doing.

They continued to see each other. But when he left to work at the Canadian summer camp they parted with a feeling of mutual ease. They said the things that high school lovers always said—they would meet again at vacation time, she would come up to M.I.T. for a weekend—all the phrases that were said automatically and forgotten just as automatically. Something valuable had existed for them but they were too young to take advantage of it.

And now it was gone.

The memory of that night was enough to set her off. Her hands began to tremble of their own accord and it took her a moment or two to still them. Desire welled up in her, desire not for Chuck Connor but for a man, a real man, a man who would make a woman of her.

Because she had already decided that she was not going to stay a virgin forever. That may have been the best course back in the dark ages, but nowadays a woman had the right to be a woman, the right to seek love and take it where she found it.

And she was going to do just that.

At high school it was wrong. At Corry Senior High School a good girl didn't let a boy make love to her. But at Clifton College things would be different. She would meet a man, a man she wanted and a man who wanted her.

And they would make love.

It was as simple as that. She wasn't going to force herself to wait, not for a wedding ring on her finger or for a declaration of eternal love. She had waited long enough, and now even the law recognized her right to use her body as she saw fit.

The next man. The next man whom she wanted would be the man to whom she would give herself. He would take her and he would love her, and he would know just what to do and how to do it, and he would make her body sing with the joy of being alive.

The next man…

She closed her eyes, thinking of the man, the man who would make love to her. She tried to picture him in her mind, tried to imagine what he would look like. Her mind conjured up pictures and her head swam with the idea of it all.

She dozed, half asleep and half awake, half thinking and half dreaming. Then the conductor shouted "Springfield!" and the train pulled into a grimy little city and finally pulled to a jerky stop at the terminal.

She practically jumped out of her seat. Her trunk was being shipped Railway Express, but she had a suitcase with her and she had a tough time hauling it down from the overhead rack. A middle-aged man helped her with it and then she was off, suitcase in hand, waiting at the platform before the train came to a stop. Her heart was beating wildly and she couldn't wait for the train to stop so that she could hurry off to Clifton.

The train stopped. She let the brakeman help her off the train and waved away the porter who offered to carry her suitcase for her. There were half a dozen cabs parked by the side of the terminal and she hopped into the first one in line, saying "Greyhound terminal" and making it sound like one single word.

"Where yuh headed, Miss?"

She told him she was going to Clifton College.

"Don't take the bus, Miss. Won't be one headed there for another four, five hours. You don't wanta wait that long, do you?"

"How else can I get there?"

"Shucks," he said, "it's only nine miles. The rate by cab is only three and a half dollars. Why don't you let me run you out there?"

"Well—"

"Listen," he said, "I'll make it three. The flat rate's three-and-a-half, but this way I can stop off in Hustead for a cup of coffee with my wife. I live out there, you see."

"All right," she said, thinking that she would have paid the three-fifty anyway if he had waited a minute more. She settled back into the seat and closed her eyes as the taxi made its way down High Street to Route 68. The driver turned left at 68 and headed out toward Clifton, and she took a deep breath and held it, thinking about the man, the man she was waiting for, the man who would make love to her.

Chapter 2

Ruth Hardy had hair as black as midnight, short black hair clipped into an Italian style haircut that bore a remarkable resemblance to the posterior of a duck. Ruth Hardy was five feet five inches tall, an inch or so shorter than Linda. She was slender, with lean but well-formed legs and taut buttocks. Her breasts were small but perfectly formed, little girl's breasts that were rounded and firm and eminently touchable.

Ruth Hardy's face was pretty, with a small red mouth and sharp blue eyes that looked straight at a person. Her gaze never wandered and she rarely blinked. She looked at people as she did everything else—neatly and precisely with no waste motion.

She was Linda's roommate. They shared a little cubicle in Evans Hall, a tiny unprepossessing room with a double-decker bed, two desks, two dressers, a closet that was not quite large enough for two people and a sink that dripped, its bowl stained from the dripping of the hard water. The water, with a high iron content typical of the region, managed to do two things—it stained the sink a sickish red-brown and it forced a girl to spend twice as much time as usual washing her hair.

Linda had just finished washing her hair. First she had showered, and in this respect the hard water was good. It left her feeling cleaner, without the slippery feeling of a softwater shower. But her hair! God, she had had to lather it a good half-dozen times before she was done. Now it hung down her back, wet and limp, as she sat in a chair in the room.

Ruth was sprawled on her bed. She had the top bunk, and both the girls were quite satisfied with the arrangement.

"I'm a sound sleeper," Ruth had explained. "This way you can give me a good kick when the alarm goes off."

They became friends quite readily. Linda decided that she liked this girl, this sharp, fast-talking little thing from New York City. And, she reflected, it was good that they had taken to each other as readily as they did. There were no fraternities or sororities at Clifton, since social groups of that nature were hardly needed on a campus of 1500. She and Ruth would be stuck with each other for the semester at least and probably for the year; it would be a lot easier to take if they liked each other.

Their conversation rambled the way conversation does between two persons suddenly thrust into a close relationship. Ruth told her that she was from New York and that she had come to Clifton largely to get away from a family with which she didn't get along well at all. She planned to major in either psychology or sociology and possibly to do graduate work after finishing up at Clifton. Linda answered that she would major in English, that she doubted that she would do graduate work in anything, since it was highly doubtful that she would graduate.

"How come?"

"I'll probably be married by then."

"That why you came to college?"

Linda hesitated. "Partly, I guess. Oh, I suppose I want to get an education, whatever that means. But I'm not the scholar type or the career type. I guess I'm looking for a man."

"Well, you shouldn't have much trouble finding a man here, not the way you look. You'll probably have to beat them off with a club."

Linda felt herself blushing.

"I mean it," Ruth went on. "All that blonde hair and a shape like yours—the guys won't let you alone. You know much about this school?"

"Just what it says in the catalogue."

Ruth laughed. "It doesn't say much in the catalogue. I know one girl who goes here, a sophomore gal named Sheila Ashley. She told me they call the catalogue *The Big Lie*. But the one big selling point they left out is that there are three men for every gal at Clifton College, Citadel of Higher Learning."

"Oh."

"*Oh* is right. It's a damn nice ratio."

Linda nodded.

"Of course," Ruth continued, "there's a difference between finding a man and finding a husband. Men are nice to have around, but most of them are interested in just one thing. Know what the thing is?"

Linda felt herself beginning to blush again and fought to suppress it. Why did Ruth have that effect on her? Maybe it was the hard, cool stare in the girl's blue eyes, the casual self-assurance that made Linda feel inexperienced and naive in comparison.

"How much experience have you had, Linda?"

Linda hesitated.

"You're a virgin, aren't you?"

She hesitated again for a moment. Then she nodded, feeling almost as though her virginity was something to be embarrassed about.

"Don't be ashamed of it. For one thing, you probably won't last that way long, not if what I hear about this place is true. And for another thing it's nothing to be ashamed of. Sometimes I wish I was a virgin myself."

"You mean—"

"I mean I'm not, obviously. New York's a pretty fast-moving town, Linda."

For a moment Linda didn't say anything. Then, slowly, she asked: "What's . . . what's it like?"

Ruth laughed, but her laughter was cool and pleasant and it didn't make Linda ashamed of her question. "That's something I can't tell you," she said. "Something you'll have to find out for yourself. I haven't been around that much to be an authority on the subject, anyhow. But from what I know about it, you don't have to rush into it. It's not as great as it's cracked up to be, anyway. It's just one of the things that happens."

They talked some more, grabbed dinner at the school cafeteria and went back to their room to talk on into the night. From time to time other girls in the same hall would drop in to talk, but Linda was too wrapped up in herself to pay much attention to them. She told Ruth about Chuck and about the night of the senior prom when she almost let him make love to her, and she told the girl about her decision to sleep with the next man who wanted her and whom she wanted. They talked and talked, and finally it was after midnight and time to get some sleep. They undressed and washed up and climbed into bed, Ruth in the top bunk and Linda in the one below it, and then, of course, they went on talking.

"We better knock it off," Ruth said finally. "Tomorrow's registration and it'll be a rough day."

"Good-night," Linda said. She rolled over on her side and closed her eyes, her mind swimming with all the new experience of the day and the immensity of all that lay before her. She decided that she wasn't really tired. Since she had to get to sleep she tried counting.

She was more tired than she thought. She was sound asleep before the fifth mental man jumped over the mental fence.

The next morning she registered for her courses. Her hall advisers, two upper class students named Paula Greene and Jeanne Randall who lived in the hall and served in an advisory capacity, helped her make out her program. She signed up for the required freshman English course, Spanish I, Western Civilization, Introduction to Sociology and Basic Biology.

The rest of the day was filled up with a hall meeting and more random conversations and bull sessions with Ruth and other members of the hall. Ruth was going to be in her sociology class and was a good deal more enthusiastic about it than she was. As far as Linda was concerned, classes were going to be a bore, a necessary evil like paying tuition. If classes were the important thing she might as well have stayed in Cleveland.

She bought her books at the college store, a batch of heavy textbooks that set her back over twenty dollars. Carting the books back to her room, she wondered how in the world they could be worth that much money to her. In all probability she would hardly so much as open them until the night before exams. That was the way she went through high school, never studying and never working and depending upon her brains to pull her through, brains and common sense. And she never got a mark below ninety in high school.

Of course, college was supposed to be a lot more difficult. You had to study and you had to do your assignments. But a smart gal ought to be able to get through on brains if she had them.

There was a dance that night in the gymnasium, a freshman mixer designed to get all the entering students into the swing of things. A group of freshmen had decorated the gym in a vain attempt to make it look like something other than a gym, but they had failed rather pathetically. A huge weird blue tarpaulin was suspended from the ceiling in an effort to lower the ceiling somewhat, but the basketball backboards and baskets were visible at either end of the room and black and red lines were painted on the hardwood floor.

And, inevitable, the place smelled like a gym. Linda wrinkled her nose when she entered the place, marveling at the way all gymnasiums the world over looked and smelled the same. When you stepped into a gym, any gym from the one at Clifton to the one at Corry Senior High School, the same smell hit you between the eyes. That good old locker room smell, but it didn't really smell so bad when you came right down to it. Sort of a man-smell, the way Chuck smelled except with the after-shave lotion left out.

There were chairs lined up on both sides of the gym and she picked one out and sat down in it. She was alone; Ruth hadn't come to the dance and there were no other girls in the hall who interested her enough so that she bothered to seek out their company.

At the far end of the gym a small combo tried to play modern jazz and didn't quite make it. About a dozen couples were dancing in the middle of the dance floor and a few dozen more pairs of boys and girls were sitting on the sidelines talking. Boys and girls in groups were making conversation too, and Linda felt slightly left out and alone in the midst of all that activity.

She looked around the room, automatically watching the men. Right here in this room might be the man who would be her first lover, the man who would change her from girl to woman. The man might be here, but still she sat alone by herself, no one talking to her, no one asking her to dance.

Across the room a tall, dark-haired boy was sitting by himself. He was wearing a pair of dark grey flannel slacks and a blue blazer with brass buttons. His tie was a thin red-and-green foulard and his shoes were white bucks in approved college fashion. He was good-looking in a quiet sort of a way but she might not have noticed him at all if she hadn't looked up and caught his eyes. He was looking at her, and when she returned the glance he looked away, as if he was guilty of peeping at her.

She continued to look at him. After a moment or so he looked at her again, and this time he did not avert his gaze. Instead he stood up and began to walk toward her. She flashed him a smile, a quick, hesitant smile that gleamed on her face for a moment and then vanished.

When he was just a few feet away from her he said: "My name's Joe Gunsway. Mind if I sit down?"

The chairs on either side of her were empty. She rather wanted him to join her and said that she didn't mind at all. He took a seat next to her and they looked at each other, knowing that it was time to get a conversation started but neither of them quite sure where to begin.

"I'm Linda Shepard," she said finally. And then, although it didn't really fit in, she added: "I'm from Cleveland."

"Freshman?"

She nodded.

"I'm a sophomore," he said. "From Champaign."

"Where's that?"

"Illinois."

"What are you majoring in?"

"Biology," he said. "Pre-med. How about you?"

"English."

They made conversation—the useless but necessary conversation of new acquaintances on a college campus, the patter that served to get two people talking to each other when they actually didn't have much of anything to talk about. The stock questions and answers: *What courses are you taking? What professors do you have? Who are you rooming with? What dorm are you living in?* And, finally, they ran out of the perfunctory questions and answers. The band was playing "Laura" and the tenor saxophonist was working out a slow, languorous melody line that pulsed and throbbed with rhythm and melody, with the drummer using brushes and the pianist laying down soft but solid chords behind the tenor solo.

He asked her to dance.

She stood up and he took her in his arms, holding her comfortably close but not too close. He danced easily but not particularly well, gliding naturally into the familiar foxtrot steps without ever showing any particular bursts of imagination.

She relaxed into the rhythm of the dance, thinking that this was the main reason that dancing had been invented, so that two people who didn't know each other at all could be at ease in the performance of a social convention, close to each other and restful with each other, moving in time to the music and not bothering with words or gestures.

He was a good four inches taller than she was and she was glad of that. Her mouth was level with his shoulder, and if she turned her head slightly she could kiss his neck. She didn't, of course, but the idea came into her head and she smiled softly to herself.

The dance ended and they walked back to their chairs. They talked more, and this time the conversation was less automatic and more relaxed and a good deal more meaningful. She told him what it was like to live in Shaker Heights and go to Corry Senior High School. He told her what it was like to come from Champaign and go to Clifton for a year. He told her about his family—his father was a doctor and he planned to go into practice with him after two more years at Clifton and four years at the University of Chicago medical school.

He had two brothers and a sister, all of them younger than he was. He liked to bowl and he played a fair-to-middling game of golf. He played checkers but didn't like it and liked chess but didn't play it well.

They sat out a lindy because he couldn't jitterbug well and danced the next dance, another slow one. He held her closer this time and she leaned a little against him, letting her perfume drift up to his nostrils. His hand squeezed hers gently in rhythm to the music and every few steps she would let her head rest up against the shoulder of his blazer.

After an hour or so they decided that neither of them really felt like dancing any more, and it would be much nicer to go down to the tavern for a beer. They walked out of the gym and down the path to the spot where he had parked his car. He held the door open and she hopped in. Then he walked around the car and got in on his side. He turned the key in the ignition and started the motor and drove the car in the direction of the tavern.

The car was a red Ford convertible, a present from his father. It was a warm night and he drove with the top down. He didn't drive fast but there was a strong breeze and the wind felt good in her hair. She breathed deeply and the air was fresh and clean, different from the sooty big-city air she had breathed in Cleveland.

She sat close to him but their bodies didn't touch and he drove with both hands on the wheel. He made conversation and she inserted the appropriate "oh's" and "uh-huh's" from time to time without really listening to what he was saying. She was thinking.

She was thinking about Joe Gunsway, about the tall dark boy sitting next to her. She liked him—that she had decided right at the start before their first dance together. She liked him, and she was busy wondering how much he liked her and how often they would see each other and what they would do together. And, automatically, she wondered whether he would be the man, wondered if he would make love to her. She looked at his hands on the wheel and wondered how they would feel on her body, touching her breasts, her thighs. She looked at him almost clinically, like a doctor looking at a patient or a mortician looking at a corpse on a table, and she wondered what he would be like.

The tavern was a college hangout studiously patronized by Clifton students and studiously avoided by Clifton citizenry. It was set up to resemble an old colonial tavern, with wood paneling and ancient-looking tables and chairs. Colonial utensils hung suspended from the ceiling—pots, pans, foot warmers, candle-molds and other weird cast-iron artifacts that Linda couldn't identify. About seven or eight young men stood drinking beer or hard liquor at the bar. Couples occupied the tables, drinking, laughing, talking and singing.

Joe led her to a booth and they sat down. From where she sat she could see the bar and the doorway. A waiter came and Joe said: "Two labels down."

She looked at him quizzically. The waiter disappeared and he smiled at her.

"What did you say?"

"Two labels down," he repeated. "That means two 3.2 bottles of Carling's Black Label."

"Why down?"

"You're not 21, are you?"

She shook her head.

"Down means 3.2; up means 6-point."

She nodded, understanding. A second or two later the waiter arrived with the beer and she poured herself a glassful. She sipped it and it was cold and good. Joe was saying something and she was answering him but most of the conversation was going over her head. She was too caught up in all that was new to concentrate on what was being said.

It was only her second day at Clifton, and here she was drinking a beer at the tavern and sitting across from her date. She was enjoying herself, really enjoying herself, and all at once she knew with an overwhelming certainty that she was going to enjoy her stay at Clifton. It was a nice atmosphere, warm and friendly, and she found herself feeling very much at home in it.

She looked up at the line of men at the bar and one of them in particular caught her attention. He was tall, with brown hair clipped close to his scalp in a crew cut and a goatee and mustache that matched his hair. At first glance the combination of crew cut and beard seemed ludicrous, but when she looked a second time they seemed to go together, as if they happened to fit this particular boy.

He was drinking some sort of liquor, drinking it straight with beer for a chaser. He didn't talk to anybody but at the same time he didn't seem to be alone. He drank laconically, tossing the liquor down his throat and following it with a sip of the beer. There was an air of complete self-assurance about him. It said that he didn't give a damn about anybody or anything.

She watched him for awhile and Joe must have noticed because he stopped talking and looked at her.

"Who's that?" she asked.

"Who?"

"The fellow with the beard," she said, pointing.

He looked around for a second and turned back to her. "That's Don Gibbs," he said.

"Who's he?"

"He edits the *Record*. You know—the college paper."

She nodded.

"The first issue comes out Friday."

She nodded again. She knew that there was a school paper

called *The Clifton Record*; it was another of those pearls of information which the catalogue supplied to entering freshmen. And, when she looked again at the boy called Don Gibbs, it seemed very logical that he would be the editor. He looked like someone important.

"I don't like him," Joe was saying.

"Why not?"

He shrugged. "I'm not sure. Nothing personal, exactly. Just a feeling. He seems phony, with that beard and all. Like he's trying to prove something."

"How do you mean?"

"Just phony."

She looked at Don Gibbs again, and this time she wanted to tell Joe that he was wrong, that the beard wasn't phony, that nothing about this boy was phony. She didn't know why but she felt that Don Gibbs was somebody very important, somebody who was going to be important to her. And as she thought about it Joe seemed to fade, as if he was just another pre-med student who would wind up going into his father's practice and never being very interesting or particularly exciting.

"Besides," Joe said, "I don't like the way he acts with women."

She looked at him, waiting for him to go on.

"He thinks he's a real hot-shot. He thinks he can... well, make any girl he looks at."

"Can he?"

"I don't know. I think he just talks a lot."

"Does he talk much?"

"I've never had much to do with him. It's just a feeling I have.

Anyway—" he smiled at her "—he's not the sort of guy you want to have anything to do with."

She nodded, thinking how wrong he was. Wrong on several counts. For one thing, she was willing to bet that Don Gibbs *could* have nearly any girl he wanted. And that he didn't talk about it, either.

And he was definitely wrong on the last score. He was precisely the sort of guy she wanted to have something to do with.

They had another beer apiece. Then Joe paid the waiter and they went out into the night, leaving Don Gibbs drinking his whiskey and sipping his beer. They drove back to her dormitory, and Joe parked the car in front of the dorm and walked around to open the door for her. He was the perfect gentleman, just as Chuck had been, and he opened the door for her and took her arm and led her up the path to the door.

He kissed her goodnight, but she decided that it wasn't much of a kiss. His lips found hers and touched them briefly. Then he released her and took a short involuntary step back and grinned at her.

She forced a smile to her lips.

"I like you," he said. "I like you, Linda."

"I like you, too." It struck her as a rather foolish thing to say, but it was true enough.

"Tomorrow night?"

She hesitated. "Yes," she said, after a moment. "Tomorrow night."

Chapter 3

The days were a whirl and the nights were a jumble and the first week was gone almost before it had started. Up in the morning and a quick shower and you put on your clothes in a hurry and rush over to the caf for breakfast. The scrambled eggs are too soft and the toast is burnt and nothing is quite the way mother made it at home. The coffee is bitter and either too hot or too cold, and you have to practically pour it down your throat because you have to get to that eight o'clock English class.

Classes. English, with a tall, balding, stoop-shouldered professor named Bruce Irvine smiling sadly at you and telling you what books you were supposed to read. *Pride and Prejudice* and *Madame Bovary* and *Crime and Punishment* and *Great Expectations* and *Daisy Miller.* Five novels plus twenty poems and you had to read them all in the one semester and understand them, and each day in class Professor Irvine would talk about the books and poems as if they were old friends, his eyes sad and his voice soft and watery.

Spanish, with Professor Esteban Moreno, who looked very Castilian with high cheekbones and a thin black mustache, and who left Spain when Franco took power in 1937. He chattered at you in rapid-fire Spanish and you had to listen with both ears and your mind because otherwise you were completely lost in no time. And he spoke better English than you did, to top it off.

Western Civ, with Hugo Mills, a stubby little man who never smiled and who was very, very clever and very, very cynical as he lectured at you on the early years of the Roman Empire. You listened to him and he was extremely interesting and extremely amusing and seemed to know everything there was to know, but you couldn't help thinking that the bitterness in his face and in his words came from knowing so much and never having done anything about anything.

Biology, with Martin Jukovsky, a quiet, mild-mannered little man who spoke so softly that you could hardly hear a word he said. But it didn't really matter and after a while you didn't bother to listen any longer, because you had already learned everything he was saying in high school and the class was a waste of time.

And sociology with Lester Birch. Gemeinschaft and geselleschaft, in-groups and out-groups, roles and patterns, variables and constants, normative norms and existential norms and you never had the slightest idea what in the world the tall, lean, fast-talking man with the piercing eyes was babbling about.

And afternoons reading in the room or at the school library, reading and half the time not even knowing what you were reading, remembering how you used to be able to lose yourself in a paperback novel and wishing you could do that instead of wallowing in all this incomprehensible and totally uninteresting knowledge.

And evenings—evenings that you spent studying sometimes, or maybe sitting around in the room talking to Ruth.

Or going out on dates with Joe.

Linda saw Joe Gunsway three more times the first week. One night they went to a movie in town and had a bite to eat at a local lunch counter. Another night they went for a long walk down one of the back roads, walking and holding hands and looking up at the stars in the sky. They walked slowly, a long way out and a long way back, and several times on their walk they stopped and he kissed her.

That Saturday night his hall had a party and he took her to it. She met other boys and girls and drank several glasses of a punch called Purple Jesus, an innocent-looking concoction of grape juice and grapefruit juice and vodka that was much more potent than it appeared to be. She got a little bit high and enjoyed herself immensely, taking everything in and noticing with approval how heavy her feet were and how happily light her head was.

After the party Joe drove out into the country, taking the same road they had walked along the night before. He stopped the car on the side of the road in the middle of nowhere and for perhaps five minutes they sat side by side, their bodies touching. Neither of them said anything.

Then he turned to her and kissed her. She felt very passionate from the punch and from the gentle blackness of the night, and when he kissed her she put her arms around him and returned the kiss with an animal hunger she had never displayed to him before. She realized with a start that the way she felt that night she would let him make love to her if he tried, and she hoped that he wouldn't try because she wasn't ready, not entirely, and she didn't want to spoil the closeness that existed between them.

There was no cause for her to worry. He kissed her again and he kissed her all over her face and throat, but after the first few times the passion went out of his kisses and was replaced by tenderness. She knew then that it would be very easy for them to control themselves. The loveplay they were going through was not the intensive frenzy that had driven her and Chuck half out of their minds, but a calm, easy-going sort of petting that never threatened to burst into flames.

When he touched her breast for the first time she felt not excited but restful, very restful. That was as far as he attempted to go that night, never fumbling with her clothing and never trying to do more than touch and feel the swell of her breasts through her dress. They sat together for a long time in the car, but for periods of time they stopped kissing and touching and sat very still together, close in each other's arms and looking out at the night. The top of the convertible was down and the air was clean and the stars bright, and she decided that it was very good to be sitting in Joe's arms and enjoying the night around her. Once when they were sitting like that his lips brushed her yellow hair and a warm, happy feeling ran through her body.

After he had taken her home and kissed her a final time he drove off into the night and she watched him from the doorway until the car turned off on a side street and disappeared from view. Then she turned away and walked very slowly up the two flights of stairs to her hall. The room was empty; Ruth hadn't yet returned from wherever she had gone that evening. She turned on the light and sat down at her desk, her head cupped in the palms of her hands and her eyes staring down at the desk top.

She sat that way for a few moments, letting her mind wander and not thinking of anything in particular. Then the first issue of *The Clifton Record* caught her eye and she opened it once again to Don Gibbs' editorial. It was a standard piece on the surface, about sixty double-column lines welcoming the freshman class to Clifton College. But a second reading revealed another message between the lines. The editorial was a subtle slam at higher education in general and Clifton College in particular.

It was, all in all, an especially mean editorial—but there was nothing you could put your finger on, nothing that would permit anyone to censure the person who had written it. It revealed that the author was a very interesting person, a very clever person.

But she had already guessed that. No, it hadn't been a guess. The minute she saw Don Gibbs at the tavern she knew that he would be worth knowing. Since then she had seen him a half-dozen times or so on campus but had still never met him.

She stood up suddenly and began to get ready for bed, undressing and washing her face and brushing her teeth. She brushed her long blonde hair until it glistened. Then she turned out the light and slipped under the covers of the lower bunk.

She decided, sleepily, that she didn't want to think any more about Don Gibbs. She already had a man, and she saw that her relationship with Joe could develop into real love. He was so gentle with her, so considerate of her.

She guessed that Don Gibbs would be neither gentle nor considerate. He might not ever so much as notice her to begin with, and if he did he would probably be cruel and sarcastic and demanding. She pictured him in her mind—the crew cut, the beard, the slight wrinkles in his forehead and at the corners of his mouth. Then the picture faded and was replaced by one of Joe.

Joe was obviously the better man for her.

But she couldn't stop thinking of Don Gibbs.

• • •

She bumped into Don Gibbs Thursday afternoon.

That, quite literally, was what happened. She was hurrying from her sociology class to the library with a pile of unreadable books under her arm and her head down. The position of her head enabled her to see quite clearly the hem of her black skirt, the white socks, the saddle shoes, and the ground she walked on.

Unfortunately, it did not enable her to see where she was going.

Halfway down the path to the library she collided with Donald Gibbs. At first, of course, she didn't know who it was that she collided with. She didn't know, for that matter, that she had collided with anybody at all. For all she knew she had walked into a tree. The shock of the whole thing sent her sprawling, with unreadable books flying off in all directions. When she looked up timidly and saw his face gazing down at her, she turned a deep shade of red and began sputtering unintelligibly.

"My fault," he said. "I should have watched where you were going."

She started to say something but before any words came out he was taking her by one arm and lifting her to her feet. Then he stooped over to pick up her books and handed them to her in a neat stack.

"Oh, yes," she said, stupidly. "My books."

"Probably. They're not mine, and we were the only two cars in the crash."

"I'm sorry. I should have—"

"Forget it."

"I didn't hurt you, did I?"

"Hardly. You all right?"

She nodded uncertainly and hesitated, wanting to turn and hurry off to the library but not knowing quite how to go about it. Before she could do much of anything he smiled at her briefly and asked: "Who are you?"

"Linda."

"That's a start. Can you give me any more clues?"

She looked at him, puzzled.

"It may surprise you," he explained, "but there are quite a few Lindas. I thought perhaps you might have some means of identification which would be a little more specific."

"Oh."

"Like a last name, for example."

"Shepard," she said, desperately. "Linda Shepard. From Cleveland."

"That's a little better. What else?"

"Like what?"

"What year are you?"

"Freshman."

He nodded. "Major?"

"English."

"Hall?"

"Evans."

He nodded again and struck a pose with one hand on his hip and the other stroking his beard. "Linda Shepard from Cleveland," he said. "What in the world do you do?"

"Do?"

"Do," he repeated. "Some people play tennis. Others paint

murals on lavatory walls. Still others climb mountains. I just wondered what—"

"Oh," she said. "I . . . well, I . . . I don't do much of anything."

He shook his head as if he was thoroughly ashamed of her but she could tell he was making fun of her. "That's bad," he said. "That's very bad. Like an oyster."

"An oyster?"

"They just sit on the bottom of the ocean. They never do a damned thing."

She waited.

"I'm Don Gibbs," he said. "*Record* editor."

"I know."

"Oh?" He seemed surprised. "You said you majored in English?"

She nodded.

"Why don't you drop up to the *Record* office tonight? I'll find something for you to do and you won't have to wander around bumping into people and feeling like an oyster."

"I—"

"The paper comes out tomorrow," he went on. "There are always too many things to do on Thursday night. I can use some help. Can you spell?"

She nodded, mystified.

"Then you can read copy and proof. Drop up any time after eight."

"I . . . I have a date tonight."

"Congratulations," he said. "Everybody should have them. Like parents."

"Parents?"

"Parents. Everybody should have dates and parents and things like that. But what does that have to do with it? The date isn't going to last until morning, is it?"

"No, of course not."

"Well, drop up after the date is over. It's simple enough, really. All you have to do is go on your date until your date isn't any more and then come up to the office. Okay?"

"Sure," she said. "I guess so."

He nodded, smiled another smile as brief as the first, and started walking off briskly. She stood watching him for a few seconds until she realized what she was doing. Then she turned and hurried to the library.

Joe was dull that night.

She realized this, and as she realized it she also realized that she wasn't being entirely fair to Joe. It wasn't his fault—the movie he took her to was a first-rate foreign film, the beer at the tavern was cold, the pizza properly spicy. And Joe's conversation was as pleasant and warm as ever.

It wasn't Joe's fault, but Joe was dull. He hadn't been dull before, and this bothered her. Because she knew why he seemed dull now. It didn't take a genius to figure out why he seemed dull. He seemed dull because, by comparison to Don Gibbs, Joe Gunsway just didn't sparkle.

She fought against this realization. When Joe parked the car in front of her dorm and kissed her, she forced herself to respond as passionately as possible, pulling him tight against her and probing his mouth with her tongue, sending his pulse racing even if her own remained quite steady.

It was a few minutes after midnight when Joe walked her from the car to the door, gave her a final kiss, and left her. It was another minute or so after midnight when she walked from her dormitory to the Student Union. First she waited until Joe's car was out of sight, because she didn't want him to know where she was going. She didn't think he would mind—she certainly didn't have a date with Don, but was only going to do some work on the newspaper. But she didn't want him asking any questions.

It was dark out, and the streetlights were spaced very far apart along the road to the Student Union. She walked quickly, hoping she looked as good as Joe had assured her she did. She was wearing her black skirt, the one she had been wearing that afternoon, with a white cashmere sweater. The sweater was very tight and not particularly warm, but the last time a girl wore a sweater to keep warm was in 1823. It did what it was supposed to do admirably. Her breasts looked as though they might peep out through the thin white material at any moment, and the lines of the bra were clearly visible when she stood in a good light. And, because the sweater was white, it made her breasts look even larger than they would otherwise.

Tricks, she thought. And they probably wouldn't do much good anyway, because Don was probably interested in her as a piece of slave labor rather than as a piece of something else. But it didn't hurt to try, anyway.

She mounted the steps of the Union building and crossed over the flat concrete stoop to the door. Once inside she realized how incredibly empty the building was. She'd been there three times a day or more since she arrived at Clifton, since the cafeteria was located in the Union, but she had never before been in it when it was empty. The building was fairly new, built just two or three years ago, and the modernistic architecture of the structure was called *Twentieth-Century Ugly* by the majority of the student body, as well as by a good part of the faculty in the privacy of their homes. The linoleum-covered floor seemed unusually wide when Linda's feet were the only ones walking on it, and her footsteps sounded annoyingly loud.

She walked up a flight of stairs to the second floor. Halfway around the building was the *Record* office; it had been one of the places on the campus tour forced upon all entering freshmen, and she found it now with no difficulty. She would have had little trouble locating it in any case, since it was the only office in the building with the lights on.

At first glance the huge room appeared to be empty. A large desk surrounded by strangely-shaped wooden tables stood at the far side of the office. A long black table lined the wall near her. There was paper in one form or another all over the place—crumpled sheets of white copy paper, folded but unfiled issues of last week's *Record,* paper bags and empty coffee cups and scraps of paper that didn't seem to possess any discernible identity of their own. She wandered into the middle of all this confusion and looked around helplessly.

Then she saw the editor's office, a separate room running off from the main room. The light was on and the door open, and she walked hesitantly to the doorway. Don Gibbs was sitting behind a large desk, staring at a sheet of paper on the desk in front of him.

He held a cigarette between the second and third fingers of his right hand and a pencil in his left hand. Another cigarette burned unnoticed in an ashtray that was already filled to overflowing with cigarette butts and burned-out matches.

The room was even messier than the outer office. There was a small brown pool of spilled coffee on the floor surrounded by more thrown-away paper. A sport jacket lay neatly folded in the middle of the floor, and near the door was a naked dress-dummy, formless and ragged, with a brassiere around the bust and a lamp coming out of the top.

Don didn't look up at first. He looked tired, incredibly tired. Everything about him looked tired, from the weary lines in his face to the rumpled, wrinkled, once-white shirt that was open at the neck and partially unbuttoned.

He dragged deeply on the cigarette and coughed. Then he turned his full attention to the scrap of paper and made some marks on it with the pencil. He studied the results for a moment, then nodded with bored satisfaction and placed the paper in the upper half of an In-Out box. Without pausing he began to scrutinize another sheet of copy paper in the same manner, marking it up with the thick lead pencil.

Linda looked at him. He was, she decided, a very complex person. She remembered the self-satisfied young man who threw down shots of whiskey with beer chasers at the tavern, the smooth and witty young man who handed her her books after she ran into him and talked her off her feet. This was a new side to Don Gibbs, this tired young man who worked without a break and seemed on the point of collapse.

She coughed nervously, shifting her weight from one foot to the other. She coughed a second time and he looked up.

"I'm here," she said. "What do you want me to do?"

Chapter 4

"Linda Shepard from Cleveland," he said. "For a while I didn't think you were going to come."

"I did."

"So I see." He stood up and walked around the desk until he was standing just a few feet from her. Then he put his hands on her shoulders and looked down into her eyes. His mouth was serious but his eyes were smiling.

"Well," he said, "what can you do besides look pretty?"

She was flustered.

"This afternoon you said you could spell. Can you still spell?"

She nodded.

He turned around and picked up a batch of sheets of paper over two feet long and four or five inches wide. He handed them to her without comment and she looked at them.

"These are galleys," he said. "Galley proofs."

She nodded, her eyes on the top galley. The print on the paper was set up like newsprint in a single column two inches wide.

"Here's how it goes," he explained. "When a reporter types up a story it goes in my IN box. I check it, rewrite it when it stinks, correct the grammar and punctuation and toss it in the OUT box. Then it goes down to the printers.

"The linotype operator gets it next," he went on. "He punches keys and presses levers and it winds up on a batch of little pieces of lead called slugs. He puts the slugs in a tray, and when he's got about sixteen inches of copy set he runs off a galley print, an impression of the type that he's got set. The guy downtown gives me two sets of galleys. I use one when I make up the papers and I proofread the other and send it back to him."

"I see."

He smiled. "Do you? That's impressive. It took me months to understand what the hell they do down there. Great business, newspapering."

He paused and sucked on the cigarette. He drew the smoke into his lungs and let the butt drop to the floor, squashing it absently with one foot. Then he looked at her again.

"What I want you to do," he said, "is proofread the copy. I'd do it myself except I've read all this copy a good ten times already and I wouldn't be able to spot any typographical errors. Besides, at this hour my eyes don't work any more and typos would go right by me anyway. Read the stuff slowly and carefully and make the corrections with a copy pencil. The outer office is lousy with copy pencils."

"How do I make the corrections?"

He groaned. "I forgot—you don't know proofreader's marks. There's a sheet outside on the bulletin board, plus a style sheet to show you what gets capitalized and what doesn't. Better check them."

"All right," she said. "How long will it take me?"

He scratched his head. "Hard to say, but it shouldn't take more than an hour tops, even if this is your first time at it. There's about six or seven galleys there—you should be done by 1:30 or so."

"When will you be done?"

He looked at her. "I won't."

"Huh?"

"I never sleep Thursday nights. It's part of the job. As soon as I get the whole issue made up with the dummies down to the news and all the copy finished I can knock off, but by then it's usually time to race down to Fairborn and pick up the engravings. And by then the first page proofs are ready at the printer's and I have to read them. With one thing or another the rest of the morning gets shot to hell and the afternoon with it, and then I take the papers and haul them over to the caf so the idiots will have something to read with their dinner. I'll get to sleep about seven or eight tomorrow evening."

"That's impossible!"

"Precisely. Great business, newspapering."

"But—"

"Every editor does it," he said. "I was managing editor under Phil Stag last year and he went through the same kind of hell. You can live through it."

"Can't anybody else do the work?"

"Not really. I've got a managing editor and a bunch of people who write bad news copy, but there's nobody who knows enough about the technical side of it or who has enough time to spare to make much difference. I wouldn't trust anybody else on make-up or head-writing, and I can't get around the job of being down at the print-shop Friday. So there's not much chance of sleeping for a while."

He straightened up. "Look," he said, "get to work on proofing those galleys. Give a yell if you need me, but I'd appreciate it if you didn't because I'll be going quietly nuts in here as it is. Okay?"

"Okay."

"Come back with them when you're done. And don't mind me if I scream or throw ashtrays against the wall or anything like that. Okay?"

She nodded and turned away, walking out of the office. She found the style sheet and the sheet with proofreader's marks on the bulletin board and took them with the galleys to one of the wooden tables. She studied both sheets of paper for several minutes until she managed to figure out what in the world they were about. Then she got down to the laborious business of proofreading the galleys.

It was a quarter after one when she walked back into Don's office, holding the batch of corrected galleys in front of her like a pagan making an offering to a god. He took them from her, glanced at them and tossed them into the OUT box.

"That was fast," he told her. "Think you did a good job?"

"If there are any mistakes there you can shoot me."

He laughed, but the laughter was strained and she knew how tired he was. "There'll be mistakes," he said. "I'll catch some of them on page proof and the others'll wind up in the paper. They always do."

"Always?"

He nodded. "We get them all the time. Nothing worth sending into the *New Yorker*, but we get some honeys. The best one that I can remember was when we were running this story about a wooded region that was partly private and partly open to the public. We had something about the public area, only we dropped one letter out of public and—"

She felt herself blushing.

"Well," he said, "thanks a hell of a lot for coming in and helping me out. You've saved me a good bit of work and I appreciate it. Any time you feel like dropping in, the office is always open and I can always find something for you to do."

"Do you want me to go now?"

"Don't you want to get to sleep? It's late."

"I'm not tired."

"But you've got classes tomorrow—"

"I can cut them. I'd like to stay around."

"Well—"

She grinned. "You just said that the office was always open and there would always be something for me to do."

"What could you do now?"

"Anything. The office is messy—I could clean it up for you."

"The janitor does that in the morning."

"You could find something for me to do. Couldn't you?"

"I suppose so." He butted the cigarette he was holding in the ashtray and looked at her again. "Are you sure you don't want to get to sleep?"

"Positive."

"Cutting classes is a bad habit to get into."

"Don't you cut classes?"

"I've cut most of my classes since the second semester of my freshman year," he admitted. "I go to about one class out of every five."

"So?"

"That just shows what a bad habit it is. I got into the habit and I've been at it ever since."

They were both smiling now. He stood up and walked out from behind the desk. "Tell you what," he began. "I guess I'm not going to be able to get rid of you for a while so I might as well make the most of it. Let's take a run down to the Landmine and grab some coffee."

"Landmine? What's that?"

"The Landmark Grill—only place in town that stays open all night. I call it the Landmine."

"I don't want to keep you from your work. You'll be up all night as it is."

"It'll only be for a few minutes."

"Honest," she said, "when I asked to stick around I didn't mean to get in the way."

"You're not in the way. I need a coffee break anyway, and it'll give me the chance to run the rest of the copy down to the printer at the same time. Besides, with you around I'll probably get done quicker than I would otherwise. You already saved me a good half-hour reading proof."

"All right," she said. "I'd like some coffee."

She waited while he scooped up the contents of the OUT box, turned off the lights in the inner office and locked the door. Then he took a soiled trench coat from a hook near the door and put it on. The coat, which looked as though it had been slept in for at least a month, made him look a little more like the stereotype of the average newspaperman. All he needed now was a crushed fedora with a press card stuck in the band. But, she reflected, the beard and crew cut just didn't fit in with the stereotype.

He flicked a switch and turned off the lights in the outer office but didn't lock the door, explaining that it was left open twenty-four hours a day in case some staff member got an inspiration and wanted to pound a typewriter. Then they walked down the hallway and down the flight of stairs and through the building and out of the door, with the building seeming even emptier and larger than it had when she first entered it.

His car was parked around the corner, a broken-down blue Chevrolet nine years old with one windshield wiper missing and one fender badly crushed. He walked around the car and got in on the driver's side without opening the door for her, but she didn't feel slighted or ignored. He was treating her as a person, an equal, and that made more sense to her than an outdated code of chivalry. She got into the car and rolled down her window, relaxing into the seat.

"I hope the car starts," he said, fishing in his pocket for the key.

"Doesn't it usually start?"

"It always starts. But with a car like this I hate to take anything on faith."

He fitted the key in the ignition, turned it and pressed the starter button. The engine gave a startled cough, as if it was outraged at being requested to perform at such an absurd hour of the morning, and turned over. Don pulled away from the curb and drove off toward the center of town.

For a few minutes he didn't say anything, driving slowly and concentrating on his driving. She felt as though she ought to make conversation, but at the same time she felt that making conversation wasn't necessary with Don. If he had something to say he would say it, and if she had something to say she would say it. The two of them didn't have to go through the rigmarole that other people went through.

She told herself that she was building sandcastles. She had no right to think that anything existed or would exist between herself and Don. He was just taking her to the Landmine to be decent, in return for the work she was doing. He probably couldn't waste his time on a freshman girl anyhow, and he certainly wouldn't waste it on her. Still, she couldn't help hoping that something might eventually develop between the two of them.

Don pulled the car up in front of an unprepossessing white frame building on the main street of town. "Back in a minute," he said, and she waited in the car, watching him walk to the side door of the print shop, his long legs covering the ground quickly in determined strides. He unlocked the door and disappeared; moments later he came out, closing the door behind him and returning to the car.

"That takes care of the copy," he said. "Now let's get something to eat."

He started the car again, parking in the lot next door to the Old Landmark Grill. The place was almost empty, with two students whom she vaguely remembered seeing around campus playing chess in a corner booth and another seated at the counter, reading a book and scribbling furiously on a pad of lined note paper.

The waitress who brought them cups of bitter black coffee and orders of scrambled eggs had permanent circles under her eyes and frizzly black hair. She recognized Don and smiled at him, a tired smile that barely got the corners of her mouth lifted before the smile was over. One of the chess players waved lazily to him and the scribbler at the counter gave him a nod.

"Everybody knows you," Linda told him.

"I'm regular here," he said.

"It's a nice place."

"It's a horrible place. But it's open. The only game in town."

She looked blank.

"The only game in town," he repeated. "An ancient joke and also the title of an excellent novel by Charles Einstein. Remember the joke now?"

She told him she didn't.

"Well, there was this faro player. Ever play faro?"

She shook her head.

"I don't think anybody ever did. I don't even know how the devil you play the game, but that's how the joke goes. There's this faro player, and he plays at this one game, and it's crooked. So a friend comes up to him and says, 'Why do you play here? Don't you know the game is crooked?' And the guy gets very indignant and says, 'Of course I know it. What the hell do you think I am?' 'Then why are you here?' the friend asks. And the guy answers, ''Cause it's the only game in town.'"

"Oh," she said.

"And that's about the only reason in the world to eat here."

She sipped at her bitter coffee and wrinkled her nose, agreeing with him.

"Clifton," he said, "is the only college in town."

"That's not much of a compliment to it."

"It's not much of a school."

They talked—about the school, about her, about him, about the *Record,* about a good many things. Not much time passed, about twenty minutes or so, and they each had a second and a third cup of the bitter coffee. From the conversation she felt he knew quite a bit about her, but she still knew that she didn't know him at all. There were so many sides to him, so many aspects. All she really knew was that she wanted to know him better and that she liked him very much.

And that she was attracted to him. Strongly attracted to him.

"Let's get back," he said finally. They stood up and he put on his coat and paid the check. They walked outside and it was colder out now, and she walked very close to him, hoping he would put his arm around her. But he didn't, and again he let her open the door for herself while he walked to his side of the car.

They were sitting in the car and he had the key in the ignition. He was about to turn it when he stopped and turned to her instead. He looked at her—a long, intense look, and she returned his stare without saying a word.

"Linda," he said. Just her name.

She didn't say anything.

"Linda—would you like to sleep with me?"

It was very strange, she thought. The question came as a complete surprise, but at the same time she was neither shocked nor startled. She was in fact very calm, and she was not blushing for a change. He continued to look at her and she kept on looking back at him, and for several seconds neither of them said a word.

Then, very softly and very honestly, she said: "I don't know."

He waited for her to go on.

"I like you," she said. "I like you very much and I'm very strongly attracted to you. Is that enough?"

"Enough for what?"

"Enough for me to sleep with you."

"I don't know," he said. "That's something you have to decide for yourself."

She nodded, understanding. "I'm glad you asked me this way," she said. "Just simple and straightforward, without kissing me or anything like that. It makes more sense this way."

"I don't like to play games. Back-seat seductions are all right in high school but they get boring after awhile. As well as uncomfortable." He said the last sentence with a grin, and she returned it.

"I'm . . . a virgin," she said. "Does that matter?"

"Not to me. It might to you."

"I'm not sure whether it does or not. I didn't plan on waiting until I got married or anything like that, Don. I came here and decided before I got here that the first man I wanted to sleep with would be the first man I would sleep with. I don't like to play games either."

"It's up to you," he said. "I like you and I want you very much. You're a very beautiful girl."

"Do you think so?"

"Of course. You should wear your hair loose, though, and get rid of that pony tail. Your hair is lovely. It shouldn't be all bound up like that."

She pulled her pony tail around and removed the rubber band. Then she fluffed her hair back in place.

"Is it better this way?"

"Much," he said, reaching out a hand to stroke her hair. It was the first time he had touched her since he placed his hands on her shoulders in the office, and now a little shiver went through her.

"Don," she said, haltingly, "if . . . if we made love, where would we go?"

"I have an apartment off-campus. I don't have a roommate and it's completely private. No one would bother us."

That was the way she wanted it, of course. No quick tumble in the back seat of a car, no furtive fumbling in a dormitory room where you had to hurry because somebody might come in, where you had to be very quiet because somebody might hear you through the thin walls. It shouldn't be that way, not the first time. It should be free and easy, with plenty of room and plenty of time.

And he would know what he was doing. He would be sure of himself, very sure, and he would know how to make love to her properly.

"I probably won't even know what to do," she said, but she had already decided what she was going to do. "I probably wouldn't be much good at all, Don. Are you sure you want me?"

He smiled. "You'll learn."

"Will you be . . . gentle with me?"

He pulled her close to him and kissed her twice, first her lips and then the tip of her nose.

"You'll be gentle," she said. "I know you will. I . . . I want you to make love to me, Don. I want it very much."

He kissed her again, a soft kiss, a gentle kiss. Then he turned the key in the ignition and pushed the starter button and backed the car out of the parking lot. She moved closer to him on the seat and their bodies were touching as he drove, more quickly this time, to the house where he lived.

His apartment was off on the other side of town, a ground-floor apartment in a brick building on Nemo Street. It was small—one room with a private bathroom—and it was only slightly less disordered than the *Record* office. Discarded clothing carpeted the floor and there were books everywhere, overflowing the bookcase and covering the top of the cigarette-scarred dresser. There were empty beer cans piled in an incongruously neat pile in one corner of the room.

She heard him close the door and bolt it and she turned to him. "Here we are," she said.

He walked to her. He took her in his arms and kissed her, and this time the kiss was not like the gentle pecks in the car. His lips came down on hers like a hawk on a field mouse and he crushed her tight against him so that her breasts were pressed against his chest. He twined his fingers in her long blonde hair and parted her lips with his tongue, exciting her more with the kiss than anything had ever excited her before. She clung to him and returned the kiss, touching his tongue with hers, moving her hands over his back, pulling him close to her.

When they parted he walked to the bathroom and turned on the light. Then he came back and turned off the overhead light so that only the soft, indirect light from the bathroom illuminated the room. He came to her and took each of her hands in one of his and looked into her eyes. She thought that it was clever of him to turn on the bathroom light and she wondered how often he had done it in the past, how many other girls he had made love to in that very room. She pushed the thought out of her mind; she didn't want to know, not now.

"Now what?" she asked shakily, knowing she shouldn't be talking or asking questions. "Do you want me to take off my clothes?"

He smiled softly. "Not now," he said, and his voice was low and husky. "Not the first time. I want to undress you."

He sat down on the bed and she sat down next to him. He held her close and their mouths fused together, their tongues working. He kicked off his shoes and stretched out on the bed and she followed suit, wondering if whoever lived upstairs would notice the four shoes dropping. Then he took her in his arms and she was taut against him from head to toe and the thought went out of her mind.

She closed her eyes. His hand touched her breast and she reached out a hand to touch him but he pushed her hand aside.

"Lie still," he told her. "Lie very still." She did as he told her and his hands were light and skillful, touching and stroking her breasts and working her into a quiet frenzy. His lips were busy planting small kisses on her eyelids and lips and ears. Then he unclasped and unzipped her black skirt and drew it down over her hips. She was wearing thin white silk panties and she wondered whether he could see her through them now, but she forced herself to remain motionless on her back, her eyes still closed, her arms still at her sides, her heart beating like a time bomb minutes away from a shattering explosion.

He began to stroke and caress her legs, starting at her ankles. He touched her knees, then her thighs, and it was with an effort that she kept herself from reaching for him and hauling him down on top of her. Every touch of his sure hands had the desired effect and excited her as she had never been excited before, and she wondered how a man could know so much about women, could be so certain of the ways to arouse her and work her into a frenzy.

When he took off her sweater she arched her back to help him and then raised her head. Her long hair got tangled up in the sweater for a second or two; then it was free and his hands were all over her, touching her. He removed her bra a second later and his hands on her bare breasts were fire upon silk. He held them and squeezed them, pinching the nipples until they were harder than they had ever been. His mouth kissed the hollow between her breasts and his cheeks burned against the sides of her twin globes of smooth flesh.

He kissed her breasts in turn, kissing with his lips and tongue, kissing and licking and sucking at her breasts and sending her pulse racing still faster. She couldn't control her breathing any longer and she was panting audibly.

"Don!"

"Shhh. Lie still."

Her panties slipped slowly over her hips and thighs and calves and the silk was smooth as a caress on her bare flesh. Now he was stroking her thighs again with one hand while he undressed himself with the other, but when she looked up and saw him lying naked beside her she was afraid again, afraid of being hurt, afraid of doing something she had never done before.

She stiffened, and he noticed it at once.

"Lie still," he said again. He touched her all over with his hands—her face, her lips, her breasts, her stomach, her thighs and her knees. Then he touched her where he had never touched her before and she opened up to him, ready for him, needing him, wanting him, her whole body and being hungry for him.

The shock of the initial stab of pain was almost too much for her and she wanted to cry out. For a moment there was only the pain and then she wanted to scream because she didn't know what to do but lie still like a corpse. Then the pain lessened and pleasure came to replace it, and her body moved instinctively with her hips rolling and her thighs churning in a slow and perfect rhythm.

Slow. Slow and gently, and almost too slow at first, agonizingly slow, with their bodies moving together and the pleasure flooding through her like water through a ruptured dam. Her hands held him to her and her fingernails dug into his back.

Faster.

His chest was crushing her breasts and her legs were like a vise around him. Her breath was so labored that breathing was an effort and she longed to stop breathing, to cease everything but lovemaking itself, to make love forever and to have forever the pleasure she felt now.

Faster.

Nothing had ever been like this, nothing she had ever experienced before. Nothing *could* be like this, nothing in the entire world; and if it didn't stop she would go crazy, but she didn't want it to stop, not yet, not ever, because God it was so good, so good and so wonderful and so unbelievable and so perfect, so wonderfully unbelievably perfectly good.

Faster.

Faster...

They ended together. It was so good that she couldn't even stop to think how good it was, could only enjoy it and love it and feel it in every part of her body and mind. Soaring all the way to the highest peak in the world and then pure peace, with him soft and limp and exhausted in her arms and so wonderful to hold, so hard against her softness, and their sweat making their bodies slippery and the tiredness leaving her completely at rest, completely at ease.

It was so comfortable. It was so good, and that was the only word for it. *Good.* Good, and there was no better and no best.

Good.

She said *Don* very softly and very quietly, and she liked the way it sounded. Then she said *Donald Gibbs* just as softly and just as quietly, and she liked the way that sounded, too.

Good.

Very good.

After a few moments he started to raise himself from her but her arms held him in place. He tried again and once again she held him.

"Don't," she said.

"I must be hurting you."

"You're not."

"Aren't I heavy?"

"I don't mind."

They remained that way for a long time.

• • •

He was standing by the side of the bed buttoning the cuff of his shirt and she smiled up at him sleepily.

"I have to go now," he said.

"Don't go."

"I have to put out a paper."

She groaned.

"Great business, newspapering."

She raised herself on one arm, ready to accompany him, but he pushed her back down on the bed and kissed her lightly on the forehead.

"Stay here," he said. "Sleep here. I'll be back as soon as I can."

She closed her eyes and her mind started to spin lazily. There was something she had to tell him, something very important, but she couldn't remember what it was.

Then she remembered.

"I love you," she said.

But he was already gone.

Chapter 5

The days that followed were a period of change, change as complete and drastic as the change that had been consummated in Don's room that night. Now that Linda's virginity was a thing of the past, it was no longer fitting and proper that she live the life of a virgin. She was a woman now, a whole and complete woman, and it was time for her to begin to live like a woman instead of like a girl.

The following evening she told Ruthie. She went to her room looking for the other girl, anxious to tell her, aching to tell somebody of what she had done. Ruth was the obvious one to tell—a girl admittedly experienced herself, a girl who wouldn't moralize or condemn, and a girl who was Linda's best friend at school.

"You didn't come home last night," Ruth said.

Linda tensed at first. Then she relaxed and a smile spread over her face.

"I know."

"Where were you?"

Linda smiled in answer.

"Oh," Ruth said. "With a guy?"

The smile grew wider.

"Offhand," Ruth said, "I would guess that something or other has been lost in the course of the past evening."

"Not lost. It wasn't worth keeping."

"Okay," Ruth agreed. "Sacrificed on the field of honor. Except I think honor's a fairly confusing term in this context. What I'm getting at is that some guy finally got in your pants, right?"

"Right."

"Who was it?"

"Guess."

Ruth thought for a minute. "Must have been that guy you've been dating. What was his name—Joe Gunsway?"

She shook her head.

"Wasn't that his name?"

"That was his name, but he wasn't the one."

"He wasn't?"

"Nope."

Ruth shrugged. "Better tell me then. I'm all out of guesses."

"It was Don Gibbs."

Ruth's eyes went wide. "Honey—"

"He's just wonderful, Ruth. I've never met anybody like him before. He's sweet and polished and—"

Ruth took a breath. "Okay," she said. "Maybe he's Central Ohio's answer to Marlon Brando. Maybe what I've heard about him is a lot of crap—I don't know. But you better be careful, honey."

"What... what did you hear?"

Ruth took a second or two before replying, choosing her words carefully.

"I've heard," she said at length, "that he breaks girls' hearts for the sheer hell of it."

• • •

Joe turned out to be somewhat harder to tell. The big thing with him, of course, was not to tell him that she was no longer a virgin, but to clue him in on the fact that she didn't want to date him any more. For a little while she considered just turning him down when he asked her out and letting him figure things out for himself, but this didn't seem to be the right way to go about it. Even if Joe wasn't the man for her, it was only fair to be decent to him. He was a nice enough guy, even if he wasn't her stick of tea.

She didn't even wait for him to call her. Instead she called him at his dorm, waiting impatiently while one of the other boys in the dormitory called him to the phone. The fact that he lived with others in a dormitory while Don had an off-campus apartment to himself seemed to her to sum up the difference between the two of them.

"Joe," she said right away, "I'm afraid I won't be able to see you any more."

There was a long, stunned silence. When he finally spoke he sounded as though someone had hit him over the head with a sledgehammer.

"Why?" he said.

"There's someone else," she said, feeling like a character in a bad movie.

"But I don't understand, Linda. I've been seeing you all the time. How could there be somebody else?"

"There is, Joe. And I'll be seeing him regularly from now on."

"But . . . how long have you known him?"

"Just one day."

"One day? Why, I saw you yesterday, and—"

"I saw him after you left last night, Joe."

Silence.

"Linda, if you've only known him one day you can't be sure he's the right guy for you. You're only a freshman, for God's sake. You ought to be dating a lot of guys so you can take time and make up your mind."

She felt like telling him that she knew Don Gibbs better after one night than she could know him if they went together for twenty years.

"Linda—" his voice was strained "—just tell me who it is, will you?"

"What difference does it make?"

"Just humor me," he said, trying to make it sound light. "I think I've got a right to find out who beat my time."

"All right," she said. "It's Don Gibbs."

"You must be kidding!"

She assured him that she wasn't.

"Linda, that guy's poison! Why, he'll try to . . . he'll be trying to—"

"To what?"

He didn't answer, and she decided that he was not only behaving like a child but making something of a pest out of himself. So she decided to get rid of him once and for all.

"To seduce me, Joe?"

He didn't say anything.

"For your information," she told him, "he already has. And it was wonderful!"

She put the receiver back on the hook before he could say a word.

Time seemed to fly by at the speed of light. For all practical purposes she moved in with Don at his apartment. Much as she would have liked to pack her clothes and move in completely and permanently, the administration of Clifton College would have looked askance at such an arrangement. Instead she had to be hypocritical about it, which was something she hated. She kept almost all her clothes and books at the room she had been sharing with Ruth and went to her dorm to change and to keep up appearances. But she spent her nights at Don's place and spent her free time wherever he was.

Friday she had awakened just about the time that Don returned to the apartment with a copy of the newspaper in one hand. She oohed and ahhed over the paper, proud of it and proud of him for having gotten it out on time. Then she wanted to make love and cook breakfast—in that order—but Don turned out to be too tired for the first and not hungry enough for the second. Instead he went to sleep and she went back to her room to tell Ruth. Then for the next week it seemed as though Don was with her all the time. Over the weekend and on through the early part of the week he didn't have much to do—the real work on the *Record* came Wednesday and Thursday and Friday, and until then all he had to do was his classwork, which he seemed to get through with his eyes closed. The rest of the time he would lounge around on campus or sit in the *Record* office or spend drinking innumerable cups of coffee at the Landmine.

Linda spent her time with him. She wanted to be with him every minute of every hour and she didn't see any reason why she shouldn't. They were in love, she told herself, and there was nothing more natural than that she should be with him as much as she possibly could.

He cut his classes; therefore so did she. He slept days and stayed up nights; to be with him she did the same. She missed the weekly quiz in Spanish Monday morning and cut an important English class Tuesday, but this didn't seem to matter at all. Don got by without attending classes—he didn't seem to study at all, either—and if she was going to be his woman she could manage to do the same.

"Kitten," he told her, "you're going to bust out if you don't start getting to classes. Admittedly the academic standards aren't sky-high around this emporium of learning, but they do flunk people out from time to time. Don't you think you ought to get to bed now so you'll be able to get up tomorrow morning?"

They were sitting over coffee at the Landmine. Linda picked up her cup and took a sip of it. Then she set it down in its saucer and grinned at him.

"No," she said. "I don't."

"You don't?"

She shook her head.

"Why not?"

"Because you're awake."

"What's that got to do with it?"

"When you sleep, I sleep. When you stay awake, I stay awake."

"Then how do you pass your courses?"

"Same way you pass yours."

"I get lucky."

"So I'll get lucky."

His face grew serious. "Linda," he said, "I'm not going to act like an angry parent, and after I finish saying this I'm not going to bring the subject up again. What I want to say first is that you stand a good chance of getting the boot from Clifton if you don't watch out. If they don't boot you for academic failure they might boot you for shacking up with me. Whether or not you get booted is your business and not mine, but I want you to know the score."

"I know."

"You're a big girl now," he said. "You have a right to make your own decisions and I'm not going to try to make them for you. As long as you know how things stand, what you do is your own business."

"Okay."

He finished his coffee. "I'm sick of this place," he said. "Want to get some air?"

"What time is it?"

He craned his neck and looked at the clock on the wall. "4:28 on the button," he said. "If the birds hadn't headed south for the winter they'd be chirping in a minute and a half. It might interest you to know that the birds at Clifton invariably begin chirping at 4:29½ in the morning."

"Always?"

"Always."

"Why?"

"Because that's when the sun begins to think about shining.

But this is all conjecture, you see, because there are no birds around right now. But we could go for a walk."

"We could," she said.

"Let's."

She got up and waited while he paid their checks. On the way out she slipped her hand into his and an automatic smile came to her face as his fingers tightened around her palm. She wanted to lean over and give him a quick kiss but she didn't, knowing that he didn't like her to display her affection in public.

They headed south on the main street of town. The air was crisp and cool and her legs were free and easy as she walked.

"Know what I feel like doing?"

"What?" she asked.

"Drinking," he said.

"Drinking?"

He nodded. "There's a whole quart of wine back at the apartment. The two of us ought to be able to empty it in a fairly short amount of time. It's not the world's greatest wine—in fact it tastes a little like goat urine."

"How do you know what goat urine tastes like?"

"It undoubtedly tastes like this wine. But there's enough there to get the two of us stoned."

"At this hour?"

"At any hour. It's powerful wine."

"I mean . . . it's kind of a nutty time to drink."

"It's a nutty time to be awake, for that matter. C'mon—let's go get drunk."

She let him lead her off in the direction of his apartment. Then he remembered that the car was parked in front of the Landmine and they turned back to get it. She held his hand tightly as they walked along.

When they got to the car she sat next to him on the seat while he turned the key in the ignition and got the car started. She wondered dizzily what it would be like to drink wine while they watched the sun come up.

"Don—do you know what I'd like to do?"

"What?"

"I'd like to make love."

"Believe it or not," he said, "it's possible to drink wine *and* make love. Not simultaneously, of course. It gets a little sloppy. First you drink the wine and then you make love. And then you drink more wine and then you make more love. And then you drink more wine and then you make more love, and—"

"What happens when you get tired?"

"Then you go to sleep," he said. "But I'm not tired yet."

"Neither am I," she said happily. "The way I feel now I could do it forever."

"Drink wine and make love?"

"Not both of them forever," she said. "After awhile I'd get tired of drinking all that wine."

The wine was as bad as he had said it was, if not worse, and although she had never partaken of the urine of a goat it seemed logical that what they were drinking wasn't far removed from it in taste. But the wine accomplished its intended objective. While its effect on Don wasn't noticeable, it got her higher than a space platform.

It was funny, she thought, the way the room was spinning so strangely. It was just a little after five in the morning and the sun wasn't up yet, and that was one hell of an hour for the room to be spinning.

"Hell of an hour for room-spinning," she warbled.

Don put down the bottle and kissed her.

"We should drink out of glasses," she said after the kiss ended, which wasn't right away.

"Why?"

"More civilized."

"Who wants to be civilized? We're pagans."

"Pagans?"

"Mad foolish pagans waiting for the sun to come up so we can worship it in the proper manner. Put down the bottle and kiss me, pagan."

She put down the bottle and kissed him. Her head was spinning like a top.

"Stand up, pagan."

When she stood up she had to lean against him for support. She clutched him and her mouth reached up for his. Her tongue darted at once into his mouth and his arms went around her to hold her.

Her blood was pounding and she felt as though she was coming apart at the seams. The wine was having a definite effect on her and it was doing more than making her dizzy. Her whole body seemed to be alive, alive and demanding, and she wanted him with a desperate passion.

"Don—"

"Take off your clothes."

He let go of her and with some effort she managed to remain on her feet. He was undressing quickly and deliberately, letting his clothes fall wherever they landed. He didn't look at her while he undressed.

She began taking off her own clothing. It was great fun, she discovered, to take off a blouse and just throw it on the floor instead of hanging it up. It was even more fun to do the same thing with a skirt.

And with a bra.

And with panties.

"Don," she said happily, "I'm naked."

"So you are," he agreed. "So am I."

She looked at him from head to toe. "Yes," she said. "I guess you are."

He was about three feet away from her but he made no move toward her. His eyes caressed her as efficiently and as effectively as hands could have and under his gaze she began to grow hot and passionate, aching with desire for him.

"Oh, God," she said. "Hurry up."

He leaned over and picked up the wine bottle. "I'll be damned," he said. "There's still some left. I thought we killed the bottle."

"Who cares?" she demanded. "Forget the wine."

"Can't forget the wine."

Her passion mounted and she rubbed her thighs together, impatient, wanting him.

"Lie down on the bed," he ordered. "On your back."

She did as he told her. He walked over to the side of the bed, the wine bottle in his hand.

"What are you going to do?"

"I'm going to drink the wine," he said gravely.

"Later—"

"I'm going to drink the wine in a new and improved fashion," he said. "You shall be the glass."

Before she could ask him what he meant by that he had tilted the bottle and the wine spilled onto her body. Most of it splashed on her breasts but some of it trickled down over her stomach and below. It was very cold and the sudden contact served only to excite her still more.

"You make a lovely wine glass," he told her.

Then he was beside her on the bed. Now she saw what he meant about drinking the wine with her for the glass. His tongue began to lick up the wine from her body, starting just below her throat. The effect of the wine on her brain and his tongue on her smooth skin was enough to drive her wild from the first second, and when he reached her breasts it was more than she could bear.

Some wine had spilled lower.

On her stomach.

Below her stomach.

He didn't miss a drop.

Then, when her passion was higher than it had ever been before, he took her quickly and savagely and exquisitely, tormenting her with the sheer beauty of his love, thrusting her higher and higher to the very pinnacle of love until she had to cry out at the moment of fulfillment.

Then her arms tightened around him and they slept like twin corpses.

• • •

She was happier than she had ever been, happier, she felt, than she had any right to be. When she was with Don nothing mattered, nothing seemed important. It wasn't just their lovemaking, though that was something that seemed to be better every single time. It was everything that passed between them. Walking down the street, sitting over coffee, proofreading copy for him while he worked on the tiresome business of editing the paper—everything was equally exciting to her. It was as though she had stepped into a new and different world, the world Don lived in. It was a world of hard drinking and hard living and hard loving, a world where the moment was vitally important and tomorrow could watch out for itself.

She couldn't help worrying about Don some of the time. He didn't seem to have any plans, didn't seem to know what he would be doing after he graduated. He didn't have to worry about the army; a trick knee that he referred to as a million-dollar wound would keep him 4-F. But he didn't plan on going to graduate school and he didn't seem to have the slightest idea where he would go or how he would go about earning a living.

"Maybe I'll grab a newspaper job," he said once. "I was glancing through a copy of *E & P*—you know, *Editor and Publisher*—and there are jobs all over the damned place."

But when she would try to get him to talk about a newspaper job he would shift the subject.

"Hell, who wants to write news copy for a lifetime? Boring goddamned job, Linda. Maybe I'll try freelancing or something. Or publishing work—go to New York and hunt up some kind of editorial assistant work. That might not be bad."

What it boiled down to, she knew, was that Don didn't want

to do much of anything. He refused to make plans for the future and he refused to worry about it, and this attitude didn't make her any too happy.

For one thing, she had a feeling that whatever plans Don had didn't include her. Time and time again she told him how much she loved him, and although he didn't exactly dodge the issue she knew that he had never told her that he was in love with her. Maybe he was and maybe he wasn't, but he didn't say anything to her one way or the other.

It wasn't hard for her to tell that he meant more to her than she meant to him. She tried to tell herself that this was natural—that she had never had a lover before while Don had had many women. But she couldn't help feeling there was more to it than that.

And it scared her. If anything happened between the two of them, if suddenly he didn't want her any more, she didn't know what she would do. He was her whole life—nothing else mattered to her, and not only didn't she see how she could live without him but she had trouble remembering how she had managed to live before the two of them were together. She couldn't imagine sleeping without him sleeping at her side, couldn't imagine living through an entire day without seeing him and talking to him. And she knew that this was dangerous.

But she worried less and less as time went by. She would live with him and love him, and in time he would come to need her as much as she needed him. She loved Don Gibbs and she was determined to wind up married to him.

But there was plenty of time for that.

For the time being she would wait. She would have him at

the *Record* office, at the Landmine, and in bed. She would spend every minute with him.

And, eventually, she would marry him. She was sure of it.

Chapter 6

There were times when Linda hardly realized that she was going to college.

This was primarily due to the fact that she was hardly going to college. While she hadn't stopped going to classes, the ones she attended were few and far between. She went whenever there was a test, after having stayed awake all night before the test cramming her mind full of the stuff she was supposed to have learned already. It was tough at first, cramming like mad all night and then staying awake the next day for the test. But she found a way to do it—coffee at first, to jolt her mind into an awake much coffee.

Then there was Dexedrine. You just took one little pill and you were awake for hours—not high, but very definitely awake with no trouble at all, your mind keen and your body in fine shape. Of course she didn't want to make a habit of Dexedrine, but taking it once a week or so couldn't hurt, and it certainly did make it easier to keep her eyes open and her mind on what she was doing.

The combination of cramming and Dexedrine kept her up to par in her courses for the next two months. But she knew inside that she wasn't getting all she should be getting out of her courses. She was missing the lectures, and what reading she was doing was confined to the more essential material. Reading somebody else's lecture notes and skipping over the underlined material in somebody else's textbook wasn't any way to get an education. It might get her through exams but that was about all it would do for her.

Well, what did it matter? She didn't much care about an education, and what Don was teaching her was a good deal more along the line of what she was anxious to learn. She knew that she was developing into a first-class bed partner, among other things, and the sort of conversation she had with Don and his friends was more broadening than the nonsense they filled you with in the classroom.

Almost all of the really interesting boys and girls at Clifton were friends of Don, or at least it seemed that way to her. The off-beat sort of kids who did things and read things and thought about things and talked about things were the kids Don hung around with, and now these were the people Linda was hanging around with. The other students at Clifton, the ones that didn't count as far as she was concerned, called Don and his friends the Bohemian set. Perhaps the term fit in a vague and inconclusive sort of away, but Linda had never heard it used by any of the people included in the circle.

They dressed to please themselves, and some of the girls in the crowd were as likely as not to wear the same pair of blue jeans and the same shapeless sweater for a week running. The boys went longer between haircuts, most of them, and some of them had beards like Don had. The traditional Ivy League uniform of three-button suit and button-down collar was missing. Nobody wore blue blazers like Joe did and shined shoes were the exception rather than the rule.

But with these people, Linda knew, dress was informal to the point of sloppiness simply because it didn't matter. They were too busy leading their own lives to concern themselves with the superficial things.

Some of them worked on the newspaper. Others painted or played the guitar or wrote poetry. Some of them didn't do anything in particular—they just belonged to the group, spending their time sitting over coffee at the Landmine or lounging aimlessly for hours at a clip on the steps of the Union Building. They played chess and held perpetual conversations and got drunk as often as they possibly could.

They were, she decided, nice people. They accepted her quite readily, probably more because she was Don's girl than anything else, but their acceptance of her mattered to her only as far as it mattered to Don. She could have made a lot more friends among the group if she had cared about it at all, but she didn't, not down deep. All she cared about was Don—he became more important to her every day.

The two of them became more close every day. Constantly she looked for signs to prove to her how much she meant to him, as if to reassure herself that their relationship would go on forever.

Inside, deep inside, she knew that there was something wrong.

They were sitting across the dinner table in the cafeteria. He held a coffee cup in one hand and a cigarette in the other. She had finished her coffee and she was sitting silently, looking at him.

"Don?"

He looked up.

"What do you want to do tonight?"

"I don't know," he said. "I think I'll do some reading for that contemporary fiction class."

"There's a good movie playing."

"Which one?"

"*Hungry Wedding.*"

"Sounds lousy."

"Rosmini directed it. It's supposed to be good."

He shrugged and took a drag of his cigarette.

"See it if you want. I'd better do the reading."

"Can't it wait?"

"Probably," he said. "But I might as well get it out of the way now as some other time."

"Then I won't go."

"Huh?"

"Well, I don't want to see the movie alone."

"Don't be silly," he said. "There'll probably be some of the group going, or you can go with a bunch of kids from your hall."

"I hardly know a soul in my hall."

"Hell, you can find somebody to go with. There's always a crowd on a Sunday night. Even if you went alone it wouldn't be so terrible, you know. In a town like Clifton you know half the theater by the time you get there anyway."

"No," she said. "I won't go."

He put down the empty cup of coffee and reached for her hand. "Linda," he said, "why don't you want to go to the movie?"

"I want to be with you," she said honestly. "If you don't feel like going it's all right. But I don't want to see the movie so much that I'd rather go with somebody else than sit around the apartment with you."

"That's ridiculous," he said. "We don't have to spend every goddamned minute together."

"I know. I just don't want to see the picture unless you come along."

"Look—I'd go, but I really don't want to see this one and if I don't get that reading out of the way—"

"It's all right," she said quickly. "I don't want you to come to the picture. I don't even want to see it any more, Don. I just—"

"Linda—"

She stopped and looked at him. There was an unfamiliar edge to his voice.

"Go to the movie," he told her.

"But—"

"Go to the movie," he repeated. "We're together all the time these days. Go to the picture and it'll give us a chance to get away from each other for a few hours."

"But I don't want to be away from you."

He didn't say *But I want to be away from you.* He didn't say anything, but he might just as well have told her that he didn't want to see her. She felt as though she had been slapped and she almost burst out crying—even though, actually, he hadn't done anything at all.

She went to the movie that night. She went all by herself while he went back to the apartment to read. The picture, an excellent Italian import, went completely by her. She kept her eyes on the screen from start to finish but she might just as well have had them shut. She didn't listen to a word or take note of a thing that happened on the screen. Her mind was too busy with thoughts of its own, thoughts she didn't want to think but thoughts she couldn't help thinking.

When she got back to the apartment he asked her how the picture was. She told him that it was a fine picture.

He read until six in the morning. He finished one book and started another—all in all, she saw him pick up and put down five novels in the time between her return from the movie and six the next morning. He read like a machine, taking in the entire contents of a page in just one glance and moving on to the next page, flipping through the book, digesting it and setting it down and reaching for the next one. She had wondered how he was able to get through school spending the little amount of time on it that he did. Now he was giving her a vivid demonstration. He was getting an entire term's worth of reading done in the course of a single night.

Six was the hour they usually went to bed. Until then she tried to get some of her own studying out of the way but it didn't work. She just couldn't keep her mind on what she was reading, and after an hour or so she gave it up and sat around doing nothing. At six she undressed and got ready for bed.

"Don?"

He didn't hear her the first two times; he was too wrapped up in what he was reading. Then he looked up.

"Coming to bed?"

He shook his head. "I want to get a little more of this out of the way," he said. "Go ahead—I'll join you in a little while."

She crawled under the covers. It was cold, and even with the blankets over her she needed something more than blankets to keep her warm. She needed Don. Alone in the bed she felt lost and unwanted.

She lay there, waiting for him to join her. But he didn't join her. He went on reading, went on flipping pages while she wanted him so badly she was ready to shriek.

At last, exhausted, she slept.

That, she discovered, was the beginning.

The rest followed in fairly short order. The closer she and Don grew, the farther apart they seemed to be growing at the same time. Every day she loved him more; every day her love became a more possessive thing. She couldn't stand to have him out of her sight, and the more she needed to be with him the more he seemed to need time to himself.

She couldn't understand it.

"I'm taking a run down to Xenia," he told her one night. "I've got to pick up some photographic stuff for the darkroom. The photographer's supposed to take care of that, but nobody else ever manages to do anything around this damned place but me. I guess this is no exception."

"Just a minute," she said. "I'll go with you."

"Don't bother—I'll only take a half hour or so."

"I don't have anything to do."

"Silly for you to come along," he said. "All I'm going to do is drive eight or ten miles, park the car, buy the junk, get back in the car and drive back to campus. You might just as well hit the books while I'm gone."

"Let me come along," she said.

"What for? You'll be wasting your time."

"What's wrong? Don't you want me along?" She tried to say it lightly, to make a little game out of it, but it didn't come out quite as light as she had intended it to.

"Sure," he said. "You can come along."

They drove to Xenia. But on the way there and on the way back they didn't have anything to talk about. She sat close to him going and a little farther away coming back, but the distance between them was much greater than the distance between the two posteriors that rested upon the front seat of the car.

Linda's only reaction was to try harder and harder to bind the two of them closer together. She cut more classes than usual in order to spend more time with Don. That Friday she didn't go to sleep at dawn, as she usually did, but stayed up to help him at the pressroom. They didn't wind up getting to bed until 7:30 that night.

The pressroom was an inky place with pieces of lead on the floor and smoke in the air. It was, all in all, the noisiest place Linda had ever been in—a linotype machine was clacking steadily in one corner, a press was creaking rhythmically in another corner, and the compositor was cursing softly and perpetually as he moved type around on the stone.

She decided that she liked the pressroom. The only trouble was that there was absolutely nothing for her to do there.

Don was constantly busy. After he had picked up the engravings at Fairborn he didn't get a minute's rest for the rest of the day. He read page proofs and the few remaining galleys. He wrote a couple last-minute heads and ironed out mistakes that continued to show up while the front page was being made up on the stone.

There was always a cigarette between his fingers and his face became more drawn and haggard as the day wore on.

"Great business, newspapering," he would say time and time again. And he would take another drag from his cigarette and get back to work.

She felt terribly useless, just standing there and watching and getting in the way. It seemed as though every time she turned around one of the men was walking into her or something, and whenever she started to talk to Don he would grunt impatiently and go on with what he was doing. It wasn't as though she wanted to interrupt him. It was just that she couldn't stand just sitting around like a corpse.

He was going over the first press-proof when she walked up to him and said: "Honey, isn't there anything I can do to help you?"

"Yeah," he growled. "Get the hell away and leave me alone."

He hadn't meant it, not really, and she knew that he hadn't meant it. But the damage was done. She felt empty inside, sure now that the relationship they had was on the rocks in one way or another and for one reason or another. That night after they put the papers in the caf and drove the ancient Chevy back to the apartment, she tore off her clothes and pulled him to the bed and they made love with a frenzy that was almost terrifying, made love fitfully and hurriedly and harshly and desperately, as if the sheer brutality of their lovemaking would be enough to bring them back together again.

But something was missing and she could sense it. The tenderness was gone from his embrace and she knew that she was not an object of love to him but a material possession. She meant about as much to him, she felt, as the car that was parked outside, as much as the pica-hole he used to measure the copy when he set up the paper. She was a thing, not a person, and he took her completely for granted.

She was willing to settle for that. Right now she would settle for anything, anything at all, as long as it meant that she could have Don. But the more she fought to keep him the more she was losing him and she didn't know what to do about it all. That night, while he slept, she lay awake. She was exhausted but sleep didn't come to her for almost an hour, even after the frenetic lovemaking, even after all the hours without sleep. For the first time she felt herself half-wishing that she was still a virgin, that all this hadn't happened to her. Everything was so much more complicated then, everything was so much easier when she wasn't in love with anybody, when she could live her own life without somebody else tearing her apart.

God, what had happened to her? Linda Shepard, the good little girl from Cleveland, here she was in a man's bed with a man asleep next to her, tired but sleepless because she loved him more than he loved her.

What in the world was wrong with her?

She reached out a hand to touch Don. He didn't stir and she ran her hand gently over his broad back as if to make sure for herself that he was there, there beside her, that he hadn't slipped out of bed and away from her while she was thinking about him. She wanted to pull him to her, to press his face between her warm breasts and love him forever.

If she did, she thought, he'd probably yell at her for waking him up.

She rolled over on her stomach, closing her eyes tight, wishing that sleep would come already. She was on her merry way to hell on a road paved with the best of intentions and she didn't know what to do about it. She was riding to hell at top speed in a jet-propelled supersonic bus with the destination sign plainly marked FIRST STOP—HELL. And the bus was in high and locked in gear.

What the hell, she thought sleepily.

At least it was a nice ride.

The bus got there the following Thursday.

It started simply enough. It was Thursday night, the night to put the paper to bed and to stay up all day Friday, the night that was the toughest night of all. She was in the outer office proofing galleys; Don was in his private office working on the editorial.

Pete Chatterjee stalked into the outer office. He was the managing editor, the man next in command to Don, a short, wiry-haired junior with a perpetual frown and an equally perpetual case of five o'clock shadow.

She looked up and smiled at him when he walked in, although she didn't like him much.

He didn't smile back. Instead he stormed into the inner office. He slammed the door behind him, hard, but the door didn't stick and swung open again.

Linda could hear the conversation through the open door.

She probably could have heard it anyway—Pete was talking in an extremely loud tone of voice.

"I was down at the shop," he said. "Jesus Christ—you only got four galleys set so far!"

"I know."

"You know what night this is? This is Thursday, damn it. How the hell are you going to put out a paper with a lousy four galleys in type?"

"The paper'll come out."

"When? Ten o'clock tomorrow night?"

"We'll be out on time."

"We'll be late," Pete said. "We'll either be late or we'll stink so bad they'll smell us in Nova Scotia. What in hell's wrong with you?"

She didn't hear what Don said.

"Look," Pete was saying, "if it was just this once it would be all right. But it's every week for the past two months, Don. Tuesday nights were supposed to be devoted to staff training sessions. When was the last time we had one of those?"

"They were a waste of time."

"Of course they were a waste of time. But the staff didn't *know* they were wasting their time, you lardhead. They thought they were doing something very important, which meant staff morale was higher as a result, which meant they were with us. You know how many staffers quit us in the past two months?"

"There's always a drop—"

"Not like this one. And another thing—the content of this rag has been getting consistently worse. How in hell did that raccoon feature wind up on page five?"

"As a favor to Ken Swinnerton—"

"You don't print thirty inches of tripe as a favor to Ken Swinnerton. Thirty inches of crap about the goddamned raccoons in the goddamned forest, for God's sake! Now who in the goddamned world outside of Ken Swinnerton—"

"All right, I was a little short."

"Thirty inches! And the page two make-up—you must have made up that page right on the stone, it was so lousy. You must have taken all the little diddley-shit that was left over and stuck it on page two and set the heads yourself."

Don didn't say anything.

"Look," Pete said, a little lower in volume this time, "I didn't come in here to raise hell because I like to raise hell. You know that."

"Decent of you."

"Don, listen to me. Look, I don't care who you lay or how often you lay her, but that little piece in the outer office is taking up so much of your damned time that you're not putting in any time on the damned paper. You—"

"Pete, not so loud for Christ's sake."

"I don't care whether she hears me or not—you're not screwing champion, you're the editor, dammit. If she's so goddamned insatiable I can get half a dozen guys to slip it to her whenever she's just too hot to take it any more. But I'm pretty damned sick of the way you spend every minute of every day with the little—"

She didn't hear what came after that. She couldn't. She was already out of the office and down the hallway to the stairs.

Crying.

•   •   •

The break-up itself came just two days after that. It was inevitable at that point. For two days she had been walking around in a sort of daze, not hearing people when they spoke to her, not hearing or talking or eating or sleeping or doing much of anything.

Lines flew through her head—the lines from *Julius Caesar* where Portia says:

> *Am I yourself*
> *But, as it were, in sort of limitation,*
> *To keep with you at meals, comfort your bed,*
> *And talk to you sometimes? Dwell I but in the suburbs*
> *Of your good pleasure? If it be no more,*
> *Portia is Brutus' harlot, not his wife.*

That was all she was, something for Don to talk to when he felt like it, to take to bed when he wanted company under the covers. And now she was just ruining his life, taking up time that he had no right to give to her.

She couldn't live with him or without him.

The blow-up, when it came, was over something that didn't matter at all. They were at the apartment, talking about a book that Don had read, and she didn't even remember later what the book was. That, she thought afterward, might give some indication of how vital the quarrel was on the surface.

Anyway, she said something, and Don said that her statement was stupid, and she said he thought he was so smart all the time, and pretty soon they were shouting back and forth, saying things that were mean, taking out everything upon each other in the guise of an argument.

But it wasn't an argument, not really. Fundamentally it was an outpouring of everything, all the hates and frustrations that had built up between them. She was letting go of all the fear and worry that had been growing day by day; he was hitting out with all the similar emotions of his own.

It was, in short, an argument that should have ended in bed. Arguments of this nature are best settled in bed, with genitals doing the job much better than words can ever hope to do. But the argument did not end in bed. It didn't get to bed, for that matter, because they broke up before they could tumble into the hay.

Almost before she knew what had happened he had told her to leave, that they were no good for each other and that it would be better if they didn't see each other any more. They weren't shouting any more—now they were trying to discuss the whole thing sensibly like reasonable adults.

And then she was saying all right, she would leave, she agreed with him, it was better that way.

And she was picking up the books and clothes that she had been keeping at his place and heading for the door.

At the doorway she faltered. She dropped the books to the floor, remembering the way she had dropped an armload of books the time they first met. And the tears spilled out all at once and she turned and ran to him, clutching at him, burying her face against his chest and soaking his shirt front with tears.

But that didn't change things. A few moments later she was on her way again, and this time she held her tears back and carried her clothes and books down the stairs and out of the building.

She walked, dry-eyed, back to her own dormitory on campus. She went to her room. Ruth was out and she closed the door and got into bed.

Then she cried. She cried on and on until her eyes were dry solely because there were no tears to come. She ran her hands over her bare body, knowing that her body would go without the touch of a lover now, that Don would probably never touch her breasts and thighs again, never kiss her and arouse her and make love to her.

When she finally slept her pillow was wet with tears. She slept for twelve hours and she dreamed that she was with Don, that he loved her and she loved him and everything would be all right forever.

When she woke up, alone in a bed she hadn't slept in for weeks, she realized that the dream was a dream and nothing more.

She began to cry again, soundlessly this time.

Chapter 7

She had always wondered what you did when the world ended. And now it had happened, finally. The whole big beautiful wonderful hopeless terrible stinking world had dissolved in one grand and glorious puff of oily smoke. So she found out what you did when the world ended.

You went on living.

Of course, for a reasonable amount of time you cried on shoulders. Ruth was there, fortunately, and Ruth's shoulder was a handy one to cry on. So she cried on Ruth's shoulder, and she told Ruth the whole stinking story from beginning to end, and then Ruth told her everything would be all right and she told Ruth everything most emphatically would not be all right, and then she cried some more.

And went on living.

For three days she lived in an impenetrable little shell. She crawled into the shell and pulled the shell in after her. In a purple fog she went to all her classes, read all her assignments, went to sleep at ten and got up at eight. But she didn't remember what the professors said in class and the assignments that she read passed directly through her brain and made no impression upon her. She had nine hours of sleep every night but she was still tired in the morning. Her sleep seemed to be one continual bad dream and there were times when she woke up in the middle of the night with terror shrieking through her heart and a scream on her lips.

After the fourth day she couldn't take it any longer. She had to get Don back or she would go out of her mind. It was terrible—she passed friends in the halls without talking to them, ate her meals without tasting her food, behaved in all like an automaton just going through the motions of living.

She waited, desperately, for Don to come to her. In the back of her mind she couldn't help knowing that he wouldn't come to her, that the only way she could possibly see him was for her to go to him, to seek him out and try to explain to him how much she needed him, how much she had to have him back.

And, in the back of her mind, she knew that this wouldn't work either. Nothing would work, and no matter how much she tried Don would be irrevocably lost.

But she had to try.

She started to go to the *Record* office one afternoon, fairly confident that she would find him there. She was on the second floor of the Union building before she changed her mind. She couldn't see him there, not with the chance of finding others around, not with the chance of somebody like Pete Chatterjee stepping in and blowing everything to hell.

Instead she walked to his apartment. The front door was open and she walked up the stairway to Don's apartment. He never locked his door; she went inside to wait for him.

The apartment was a mess again—piles of debris all over the floor, the bed unmade and the room generally filthy. Without thinking she began to clean it up, to put the books where they belonged, to hang the clothing in the closet and stuff the dirty clothes in his laundry bag. She threw out the garbage, piled the scraps of paper neatly on his desk, made the bed and generally created order out of chaos. It gave her something to do, and at the same time it made her feel close to Don again the way she had felt when the two of them lived together and when cleaning the apartment was part of her daily routine.

When she had finished, when the apartment was as clean as it had ever been, she sat down in a chair to wait for him.

He came home an hour or so later. He walked into the apartment, not seeing her at first, not even seeming to notice that the room had been cleaned or anything. Then he looked over at her and a strange expression appeared on his face.

"What the hell—"

She saw at once that he had been drinking. His eyes were a little bit bloodshot and out of focus and his step wasn't as sure as it normally was. He could walk and talk straight even after hitting the bottle hard for a long period of time, but she knew him well enough by this time to know that he was more than a little drunk.

"I wanted to see you," she said.

He lit a cigarette, dragged on it and expelled the smoke from his lungs. Then he kicked off his shoes and sat down on the edge of the bed. He didn't say anything to her.

"I had to see you," she went on. "I . . . I need you."

"Like you need a broken collarbone."

It wasn't working at all. What did she have to do—get down on her knees and crawl to him?

"Don—"

She broke off after saying no more than his name. Now that she was here and he was with her she didn't know what to say.

She had an insane desire to run to him and throw herself into his arms, but she felt that if she did he would probably slap her face.

"Linda, you shouldn't have come here."

She looked at him but his eyes were turned downward as if he didn't want to look her in the face.

"There's nothing left for us," he said. "I'm sorry for any pain I've caused you, but the only thing you can do now is get along without me. If we go on it'll just be that much worse for both of us."

She opened her mouth and closed it again without saying anything.

"We just aren't right for each other," he said. "I'm too old for you and you're too young for me. I should have left you alone to begin with but I wanted to let you make your own decisions. Maybe they were the wrong ones, I don't know. But if we get involved again it'll be that much worse."

"Don—"

"Please," he said, and he sounded very tired all of a sudden. "Please, Linda. I wish you'd go now. If we keep away from each other it'll be better for both of us."

She took a deep breath and held it as long as she could while he sat silent upon the edge of the bed. Then she let the air out of her lungs, slowly, and began to speak.

"Just one more time," she said. "Just make love to me one more time even if it's the last time. I want you, Don."

For a moment he didn't say anything.

"See how shameless I am?" she went on. "But I can't help it, Don. I need you and even if all it is is one more night or one more hour I want to have you."

He looked up.

"No," he said.

"I—"

"Damn it, can't you get it through your head that *I* don't want *you*? I want this to be over once and for all, Linda. I wish you'd just get the hell away and leave me alone."

"Please, Don—"

"Get the hell away from me," he said, his voice low and angry. "If you're so hard up go back to your dorm and find yourself a candle."

She went back to her dorm, but not to find a candle. She went back, walking blindly and not looking where she was going. Don didn't want her, not at all, not even for one last bounce in a bed, and she knew now that the world had definitely ended, that there was nothing left for her, nothing at all.

She undressed before her mirror, taking a long slow look at herself, studying her firm breasts and flat stomach, handling herself all over to assure herself that it was a good body, a desirable body, a body that men would want to make love to. Her hands cupped her breasts and held them like burnt offerings to the image in the mirror, and she studied her reflection and wished that the hands that held her breasts were Don's hands instead of her own, that Don's eyes instead of her own eyes were busy studying the curves and contours of her body.

She didn't want to go to sleep that night. But she didn't want anything else, either.

She knocked herself cold with four sleeping pills and slept through all her classes the next morning.

Joe Gunsway called her the next day. She went to the phone convinced that the call was from Don even though she knew he would never call her, went to the phone on the run and grabbed the receiver and held it to her ear, saying *Hello* right away and praying that Don's voice would come to her over the wire.

But the voice was Joe's.

"I wanted to get in touch with you," he said. "I . . . heard that you and Don broke up."

"That's right," she said, amazed how calm she sounded to herself. "We broke up."

"I . . . well, I wondered if I could see you this evening."

At first she didn't answer and he repeated what he had said, thinking that she hadn't understood him. But she had understood him, all right.

And she couldn't think of anything she wanted to do less than go out with Joe Gunsway.

"No," she said. That was all—just the one word. She wasn't in the mood to go into details.

"Linda—"

He stopped. She waited for him to go on.

"Linda, why not?"

A logical question, she thought. It deserved an equally logical answer.

So she said: "I don't want to see you."

"But why?"

Because you're too good for me, she wanted to say. *Because I'm Don Gibbs' cast-off whore and nothing more than that. Because I'm a lousy little tramp and you're a nice square guy and you can do better than me.*

But she didn't say that. Instead she said: "I just don't, Joe. Please don't call me any more."

And she put the receiver back on the hook. He called again, of course, as she must have known he would. This time she didn't talk to him at all. As soon as she knew that it was him again on the phone she replaced the receiver and broke the connection again.

He didn't call any more after that.

For the next week she didn't do anything.

It is not easy to do nothing at all. As a matter of fact, it takes either a great deal of concentration or a great deal of lack of interest in the world. Linda didn't have a great deal of concentration—concentration in general was too much for her just then. But she possessed an enormous capacity for lacking interest in the world.

Nothing mattered any more. It was as simple as that.

There were quite a few things she did not do. She did not go to classes. She did not open a book. She did not even read the *Record* when Don deposited a stack of copies on the table in the caf Friday night.

She ate, but only when she was starving and then only enough to keep her alive. She slept, but only when she was so exhausted that she couldn't stay awake any more. She woke up, but only when she had slept as long as she possibly could.

She didn't speak to people if she could possibly avoid it. She didn't go for walks or look at the scenery. In short, she did as close to nothing as she possibly could while still eating and breathing and sleeping enough to keep alive.

She would sit in her room for hours on end, just staring at the wall like a schizophrenic or looking out the window without seeing anything on the outside. She would lounge on the steps of the Union building along with the other people in the group, but she would sit there for hours on end without exchanging a word with one of them, without listening to what they said, without doing anything in particular.

During that week she hardly even thought about anything.

That was funny, in a cockeyed sort of away. Every once in a while her mind would start on one cycle of thought or another, but before long she would be thinking about Don again and she would get all fouled up. It was easier not to think than to think about Don.

So she quit thinking.

Ruth tried to pull her out of her depression. Ruth wasn't around the room much—she was spending more and more time up at Sheila Ashley's room—but still she talked to Linda whenever she saw her and tried valiantly to cheer her up.

Needless to say, it didn't work.

Nothing worked.

The trouble, she decided, was that she no longer seemed to want anything. She wanted Don, of course, but wanting Don was like wishing for wings. If she had wanted anything in particular she might have been able to shake the mood of depression that nestled around her neck like a black albatross.

As it was, she didn't want a thing in the world. And that was worse than wanting something she could never have.

Finally—and it took over a week—she found something she could want.

A man.

It wasn't quite that simple. She was standing nude in her room again before her mirror, looking at her body, touching herself and remembering Don's touch. It occurred to her that her body was a very good body, a body that men ought to want. And it also occurred to her that even if Don no longer wanted her body, somebody else might want it.

It wasn't Don's private property any more, that body of hers. If it no longer belonged to Don, there wasn't much sense in keeping it out of circulation until the end of time. Why not let somebody else have a crack at it? Don had told her to go back to her room and find herself a candle. But another man would do her a lot more good than a candle, that was certain.

She gave the matter a lot of concentrated thought while she stood nude before her mirror and gazed upon the reflected breasts and belly and thighs. She imagined a man with a blank face, a shapeless nonentity, a man who would touch her and arouse her and take his pleasure with her and ultimately satisfy her, and her mind made itself up after a while.

She got dressed. She put on the white sweater she had worn to the *Record* office that first time, but now she omitted the bra. She would make things easier for whoever she selected as her human candle.

She slipped a skirt on without bothering with panties underneath it. The skirt was a dark green and it contrasted nicely with her blonde hair and with the white sweater. She didn't bother with socks but pulled a pair of dirty white tennis shoes onto her feet and tied them quickly.

Then she left the dormitory. She wandered aimlessly around campus for about half an hour, not knowing who or what she was looking for, not knowing where to search for the man who would serve as Lover Number Two. For a moment she considered hunting up Joe Gunsway—he certainly wanted her, and he'd be more than grateful for a chance to maneuver her into a horizontal position. But she decided that she didn't want Joe. Joe represented a potential emotional involvement, on his part if not on hers, and she didn't want to find anybody who would fall in love with her. She just wanted somebody to take her to bed.

It was cold out—in a week or so it would probably be snowing, but now the ground was blanketed with covered leaves and the night air was clear and cool and quiet. She wandered around, getting halfway into town at one point before she turned and headed back toward the campus.

She was looking for a man. And, ultimately, she found a man.

His name was Jim Patterson.

He was a junior, she knew, and he was majoring in economics. She knew him enough to say hello to—he was one of the vague members of the Group—the gang of boys and girls that Don hung around with. He was short and wiry, with a goatee that was always neatly trimmed and eyes that seemed to look through a person.

When she saw him he was walking alone on the way back to his dormitory. He had a few books under one arm and there was a pipe in his mouth. He didn't see her at first, and she had to run up to him before he noticed her.

"Jim!"

He turned and looked at her, his face blank. "Hi," he said. "Where are you headed?"

"Nowhere special."

She looked at him—a bold, purposeful look. He wasn't a moron; he knew what had happened between her and Don, knew what she wanted when she looked at him like that.

"Wait a minute," he said. "I want to get rid of these books. I'll be down in a second."

She waited at the side of the dormitory while he walked up the fire escape. While she waited she wondered what would happen, whether he already knew what she was after or whether she would have to be more obvious about it.

When he came down the fire escape with a blanket under his arm she knew she didn't have to worry about it any more.

"Let's go for a walk," he said. She nodded and let him take her arm. They walked along silently across the campus toward the golf course.

Clifton's excuse for a golf course had greens that looked like fairways and fairways that looked like rough. This, of course, was perfectly all right, since no one had attempted to play golf on the six-hole weed patch since Grant had been elected president of the United States. The physical education golf classes played on the course at Xenia Country Club. The golf course at Clifton had one use and one use only, but that use was enough.

It was a golf course with hazards, of course. The hazards consisted of the pairs of bodies that blanketed it from tee to green on warm nights. There was a legend that the president of Clifton had once walked the length of the golf course on a pitch-dark spring evening. At one point he stepped on someone. The boy who had been stepped on thanked him profusely and went back to what he had been doing.

There were those who swore the legend had a firm basis in fact.

The course was relatively empty that night, however. It was late and it was cold and the two of them had as much space as they could possibly have wanted. Without saying a word Jim spread the blanket out on the ground and the two of them sank to the ground and sat on the blanket side by side. For several seconds, neither of them made a move or said a word. Then, as if by some prearranged signal, they turned to look at each other. It was very dark—Linda could barely make out the boy's features.

But it didn't matter what he looked like.

"You're very pretty," he told her. The words were automatic—mere formality to go before the more serious business of the day. Gratefully she snuggled closer to him and his arms went around her.

They kissed. It was a passionate kiss right from the start, with both of their mouths open and both of their tongues urgent and demanding. She pressed close to him so that he could feel her breasts through the sweater, rubbing herself against him while she touched his tongue with her own.

When the kiss ended she stretched out on the blanket and he

lay down beside her. She lay on her back so that he could touch her breasts, and with her eyes wide open she watched the few stars that were out that night. His hands, through the thin sweater, were warm and insistent as he manipulated her breasts expertly and she felt her nipples hardening into firm little rubies.

She lifted herself up on her elbows and helped him take off her sweater. His gasp of pleasure at the sight of her two perfect breasts made her feel warm inside, warm and wanted and desirable. The ache that had been present within her since Don had refused to sleep with her now seemed to evaporate as his hands stroked her breasts and excited her as Don's hands had excited her not so long ago.

Then he removed her skirt, folding it neatly and placing it on the blanket beside them. His hands touched her where no hands had touched her in too many days and she writhed under his hands, wanting him, ready for him.

She unbuttoned his flannel shirt and he took it off. She touched him and held him and his breathing was becoming faster and harsher now and she knew how much he wanted her, how much he had to have her, and her heart swelled with the pleasure she derived from his need just as it pounded with her own physical need.

Then he was naked, ready for her as she was ready for him. She felt ridiculous with her tennis shoes still on her feet and kicked them off impatiently, then drawing her feet up and making herself ready for him. There was no time to waste on loveplay, no time to waste on kisses and caresses, no time for anything but pure sexual pleasure.

"Hurry!" she begged him.

He took her and her body slipped at once into the now-familiar rhythm. Her hips churned as her arms locked around him and pressed him against her. She felt almost alive again, alive for the first time in weeks, and she wanted to make the moment last forever, to make him stay there until the end of the world, loving her savagely and passionately forever.

He reached his climax before she did and she feared for a moment that he would leave her before bringing her the release she craved so desperately. But her fears vanished the next second as he stayed with her, moving with her, straining with her, until she floated higher to the top and finally received the gift of peace that was so essential to her.

Then they lay together very still. It was over now—they had made love and now they could part like the proverbial two ships that pass in the night. Now she had had her pleasure; she wanted only to be alone.

He seemed to understand.

Awkwardly they separated and began dressing. She put on her sweater and skirt, then her tennis shoes, wondering as she did so why she felt absolutely no emotion toward Jim Patterson. She felt that she ought to love him or hate him or something, but instead there was no emotion at all, nothing that lingered after the so necessary orgasm had come and gone.

They stood up and he folded the blanket and put it over his arm, letting her take his other arm as they walked back to the campus. They parted at the edge of the golf course—their dorms were in different directions and there seemed to be no need for them to walk together any further. She went straight to her room without a backward glance at him.

It wasn't the same as it had been with Don. It was sex, nothing but sex, and it wasn't the same as what she had enjoyed in the past. It was the quiet and random breeding of animals in the privacy of a barnyard. The only purpose was physical satisfaction, the only emotion was an indefinable feeling of camaraderie.

But, she thought as she undressed for bed, able to sleep at last, it was surely better than nothing.

Chapter 8

Nothing spreads like good news.

This is a well-known fact. The best news gets around the quickest, and on a campus the size of Clifton's news of almost any sort travels at the speed of light. There is a saying that, if you have an abortion in Schwerner Hall, the news will reach Buchanan Hall on the extreme side of the campus before you can flush the fetus down the toilet.

This is very probably true.

The news that a pretty freshman by the name of Linda Shepard was currently available for fun and games was an item which belonged in the category of special priority good news. It wasn't exactly as though Jim Patterson was one of those boys who boff and tell. He didn't run out and scream the happy news to the rooftops. Neither did he tell everybody he met. He simply revealed the fact to a few select friends.

Who in turn revealed it to their friends.

Who in turn relayed the message to their own friends.

And, before too long, Linda Shepard was one of the most popular girls in the freshman class.

• • •

Linda's first knowledge of her new-found popularity came with a phone call the following afternoon. There was a boy on the other end of the line, a boy named Leon Camelot.

"Hello," he said. "My name is Leon Camelot."

"Oh," she said, which was as much as she could say, since the name Leon Camelot meant absolutely nothing to her at the moment.

"There's a good movie playing in town tonight," said Leon Camelot.

"There is?"

"Uh-huh. Would you like to see it with me?"

Why not? she wondered.

So she said: "Why not?"

"Swell," said Leon Camelot. "I'll pick you up at 7:30."

Leon Camelot picked her up at 7:30. Leon Camelot turned out to be a tall beanpole type with glasses and a rather bulbous nose. He told her that he was majoring in physics and that he planned to go to graduate school at M.I.T. At the time she could imagine nothing duller than majoring in physics and going to graduate school at M.I.T., but she didn't tell him this.

On the way down to the show she sat next to him in the front seat of his brand-new Rambler sedan and listened to him talk about the miracles of the modern physical world. He seemed to know everything there was to know about relativity and quantum theory, and while this didn't make for the liveliest conversation in the western world, it was something of a change to sit next to an expert on such vital facets of everyday living.

The movie, contrary to Leon Camelot's report, wasn't much to sit through—the standard Hollywood drivel complete with the phony happy ending. Instead of watching the actors mince around on the screen she relaxed in her chair and wondered why in the name of Einstein Leon Camelot had called her for a date. Time, she decided, would tell. And whatever it was, it was something to do.

The movie ended.

Everything does, if you give it time. Even a movie like that one. Anyway, it ended, and after it was over Leon Camelot took her by the hand and led her out of the movie theater.

"Wanta coke or something?"

She shook her head.

"Wanta go for a ride?"

"Okay," she said. She didn't have anything better to do, just books that she didn't want to read and studying that she didn't intend to bother with. Why not go for a ride with Leon Camelot?

They went for a ride. The Rambler was a fine machine and Leon Camelot knew how to drive very well. Linda wondered dimly whether his ability behind the wheel was in some way due to his prowess in the world of physics. It was something to think about anyway.

Leon Camelot, it turned out, not only knew how to drive but also knew how to park. Subtle he wasn't, but all of a sudden the car was parked on a shady lane unsullied by streetlights. It suddenly became quite clear to her why Leon Camelot had called her for a date. She wanted to say something bright and clever, but all she could think of was how in the world were they going to do it in the car.

So she said: "'How in the world are we going to do it in the car?"

"It's a Rambler," he explained.

"So?"

"The seats go down."

"That's nice," she said. "The seats go down and so do I."

He blinked, and his bulbous nose seemed more bulbous than ever. She turned on her seat and looked up at him, waiting for him to begin. Not once did it occur to her to refuse to make love with him. It was as though she had found her role in life—the question of her own desires didn't enter into the picture.

But Leon didn't seem to know what to do.

"Leon—"

He stared at her and blinked again.

"Didn't you ever—"

"A few times," he said. "But never with a girl. I mean . . . never with a girl from school or—"

He broke off, looking somewhat bewildered, and she waited for him to say whatever he was trying to say.

"With prostitutes," he said. "Down at Newport there's a place some of the guys go to some of the time. But I never did it with a girl that I knew."

He looked so sincere that she didn't know whether to laugh or cry. For a moment it occurred to her that she was being called upon to double in brass for a Newport whore but she didn't let the thought worry her.

"Leon," she said softly, "don't you know what to do?"

"I know what to do. I just don't know how to get started."

He was approaching the problem like a problem in theoretical physics, and that wasn't the right way to go about it. "You could begin by kissing me," she suggested.

He followed her suggestion. At first the kiss wasn't much more than the pressing of one pair of lips against another, but after a little practice she was surprised to discover that Leon Camelot was learning quickly. Despite herself she felt her heart quickening, found herself getting excited as his arms tightened around her.

"Let's put the seats down," she said.

They put the seats down. The seats in Leon Camelot's Rambler evidently hadn't been down in quite awhile—which was more than could be said for Linda—and the time it took to get the car ready for battle almost killed her mood. But he kissed her again and she got back into the spirit of the occasion.

"Unbutton my blouse."

He performed like a highly skilled robot, but once her blouse and bra were off and he was fondling her breasts clumsily but effectively she was able to forget where she was and who she was with. He kissed her breasts, not skillfully as Don had done but with a certain amount of passion, and she didn't have to manufacture excitement. She was quite thoroughly aroused.

She took off her skirt and panties without any prompting and he had the sense to follow suit. There was something strange about lying around stark naked in a parked car but before long she found herself used to the idea.

Now that the two of them were naked Leon Camelot's hands took on a new assurance as he caressed her and kissed her and drove her half-wild with hunger. Either he learned quickly or he did a lot of reading, she thought.

Then she didn't bother thinking any more.

There were better things to do.

And, once they really got down to business, her brain was

spinning around much too quickly for any thoughts to germinate in her head. They made love quickly, feverishly, hectically, and at one point she was afraid that the rhythm of their bodies would start the car rolling along the lane.

Then, eventually, it was over. The customary feeling of relief was present as the usual aftermath, but for the first time she felt acutely ashamed of herself, conscious that what they had done was wrong, even inexcusable. As she dressed she found it impossible to look at Leon Camelot, and on the drive back to the dormitory she stayed on her own side of the car, careful to avoid touching his arm, careful to keep from any additional physical contact with the boy.

At her dorm he asked her if he could see her again and she told him maybe sometime, that he could call her some evening next week if he felt like it. She said the words automatically, knowing all the while that he would not call and that if he did she would not see him. The experience had been nothing more than just that to him, she felt, nothing more than an experience not far removed from previous excursions to the Newport cathouses. It wasn't likely that he'd be particularly anxious for a repeat performance.

As for herself, she already knew what the affair was for her. Just part of a pattern, a pattern that was going to be repeated again and again, over and over, on and on and on and on. She walked up the steps and down the hall to her room, undressing for bed, anxious to sleep. First, though, she had to take a shower. She felt truly unclean for the first time in her life.

The shower didn't help. She scrubbed herself over and over

with no discernible effect. Finally she gave up and went back to her room and crawled into bed.

Her head started spinning. She had to get up and race down the hall to the bathroom again, where she was violently sick to her stomach for several minutes.

It was almost dawn before she finally passed out and slept for sixteen hours.

Leon Camelot was followed by Frank Willet, who in turn was followed by Jackson Rice, who paved the way for Nick Bingle, who gave way to Roy Swinnerton.

Thus the days went by.

And the nights.

It made perfect sense to her. She was the tramp of Clifton College, the little girl who could be counted on for a tumble on the turf or a roll in the hay whenever a guy needed something female to take his mind off the pressing business of books and tests and classes. She had more dates than she wanted, but dates weren't the only source of sexual satisfaction. There would be a date in the early part of the evening, a date that was nothing more than the prelude to a scramble in the back seat of a car. She found in the course of it all that if you weren't particularly choosy it wasn't at all difficult to make love in a car, even a non-Rambler without descending seats to simplify matters. Or, if something more than automotive sex was on the evening's program, there was always the motel down the road where any couple was automatically man and wife and where the proprietor didn't care what went on as long as he got his money in advance.

After the date, her companion of the evening would drop her ceremoniously at her door and wish her goodnight. Then she would troop down to the Landmine for coffee, waiting for someone to come and pick her up. And there was always somebody willing, somebody who would take her to still another place and make still more love to her.

Why not?

What else was she good for?

Nothing, she would answer herself.

Still, she couldn't help feeling sick inside from time to time, sick and empty and wasted. She had stopped writing her weekly letter home, but mail from the family still arrived, pathetic and hopeless letters that revealed how blissfully unaware her mother and father were of the sort of life she was leading.

Well, the hell with them. What they didn't know might hurt *her,* but it surely wouldn't hurt them. Every once in a while she forced herself to write a letter to them, a silly and vacuous letter full to the brim with news of events that had never happened, a letter loaded with the stuff and nonsense that she knew they wanted to hear from her. Just so it made them happy, she told herself. Someone in the family might as well be happy.

She gave up classes entirely. Midterms were over and the close of the first semester was coming with its load of exams. She let it come and go, not even going to two of her finals. The others she attended and failed gloriously.

It didn't matter.

Nothing mattered.

Nothing mattered at all.

She went home Christmas vacation. She went home and lied

and pranced around and acted like a veteran trouper, and no one in the family could possibly have suspected a thing. It was rough, that two-week vacation without a man, and on the night before she was due to go back to school she called up Chuck Connor and got him to take her to a drive-in. She looked forward to sleeping with Chuck, looked forward to completing at last something that should have been completed long ago.

But fate somehow decreed that she confine her sex life to the Clifton campus. Her period came in the middle of the movie, so as far as Chuck ever knew she was still a virgin.

Back to school.
    Back to the old routine.
    Back to the sack.
    It was the first week in February when she discovered it was possible and rather pleasant to make love in a dormitory room in the middle of the afternoon. It happened in Lee Colestock's room in Buchanan hall and it was a very enjoyable experience for all concerned. All, in this instance, happened to be Linda and Lee.

Ruth tried to talk to her. It was, Linda thought, a little late for the brunette to start playing the dutiful roommate, but Ruth seemed sincerely concerned for her.

"Look," she said, "you're not in so deep that you can't stop. You can get to work and pass your courses and keep away from men and—"

"I couldn't possibly pass my courses."

"You could if you spent enough time on them. If you quit sleeping around and—"

"I couldn't possibly quit sleeping around."

"Of course you could. If you really wanted to—"

"But I *don't* want to."

And that settled that.

Don wouldn't see her. She tried to see him two or three times, just so that the two of them could knock off a quick one for auld lang syne, but he wouldn't get near her. He seemed disgusted with her, but it was more than that. It was as if he didn't want to see her because being with her made him feel ashamed of himself.

Well, she could live without Don. There were plenty of other fish in the pond. And she was developing into a far-better-than-average fisherwoman. It was amazing how adept a girl could get at the grand game of sex when she had a lesson or two every day of the week.

There were a good many ways to make love, she was discovering. There were an almost infinite number of variations on a basically sound theme, and variety was making life quite a spicy affair.

It was a good life, all in all.

Except during the bad moments.

The bad moments were a perennial occurrence. Every once in awhile, every couple of days, the whole twisted pattern of her life would stand up on its hind legs and stare her full in the face until she couldn't stand it any more. Those were the bad moments, and after they had happened a few times she recognized these periodic fits of depression for what they were and learned to cope with them.

It was a good thing she did. The first really bad moment put her so far down that she actually went so far as to draw a razor blade over her left wrist three times, experimentally, not quite ready to slash her wrists and bleed to death but more than ready to consider the prospect.

Then she learned what to do when things got so bad that she felt like killing herself. It was a simple way out, when you stopped to think about it. You didn't kill yourself and you didn't crawl in a hole and pull the hole in after you and you didn't just sit around and mope or look for a shoulder to spill tears on.

You picked up a bottle and drank.

It wasn't at all difficult for her to get hold of a bottle. According to the law she couldn't drink anything stronger than 3.2 beer until she was twenty-one years of age, but there were a lot of things that the law said which didn't quite jibe with her own personal behavior patterns. Why in the world should her drinking coincide with the norms prescribed by law?

No reason, really.

So she drank.

Boys bought the liquor for her. She didn't exactly hit the bottle like a full-fledged refugee from Alcoholics Unanimous, and all she needed was a fifth of liquor a week in order to be sure of staying reasonably sane on the surface.

That was all.

She drank gin because it tasted like medicine. Every time one of the bad moments came she would go off to her room and drink just enough gin so that she didn't feel rotten anymore. She never got high, never got happy-drunk, and very rarely got so stoned that she passed out. Just enough gin to give her a little edge on the world was all she wanted. She poured the gin from the bottle into a paper cup and drank it neat, wrinkling her nose each time because she loathed the taste of the gin.

A psychiatrist might have said that she picked gin to drink because she liked it less than any other form of liquor. But there was no psychiatrist handy to clue her in on the reason for her choice of beverage. She drank gin because she felt like drinking the gin.

Period.

End of report.

Speaking of periods, she missed hers.

That was a trauma. It happened in February. It was due on the eighteenth of the month, and then the twentieth of the month rolled around without anything happening that was supposed to happen. She felt like reaching for the razor blade. In a panic she went to Ruth and told her and the two of them sat on pins and needles worrying and shaking and wondering what in the world to do.

They didn't do anything.

And, happily, two days later there was nothing to worry about. But the false alarm was enough to throw a good scare into her.

Not enough of a scare.

It made her drink—she poured down a lot of gin that night after there was no longer anything to worry about and she cried like a baby.

Four days later she spent the night in a motel with a boy whose name she forgot before daybreak.

By this time she had lost count of the men she'd slept with. It was getting pretty hard to keep track. For one thing, there had been a certain percentage of repeats—two or three time winners.

Besides, who counts?

All she knew was that she was a tramp, a slut, a roundheeled girl no good for anything but sex. She would flunk out of school and wind up screwing her happy way through life until she finally died and they put her in a box and shoveled her into a hole. This, while it made her drink during the bad moments, made her almost happy the rest of the time.

In a sense, she thought, she was lucky. She had found her own particular niche in life, if nothing else. Other girls might go for years without finding the thing they were best suited for, but not Linda Shepard.

She knew what she was cut out for.

Yep.

By the middle of March there was very little she hadn't done and very few men she hadn't done it with. The school's administration must have known about her but if they did they didn't say anything. Her hall advisors couldn't have helped knowing but did just as little to straighten her out.

She would do anything, anything at all. Boys went out of their way to think up new perversions to practice with her. One of them beat her with his belt, hurting her and torturing her until she had to scream with pain, and finally making love to her in the most agonizing way known to modern man.

She wasn't surprised in the least to discover that she enjoyed it.

She went on. Her own mind was inventive enough and she frequently came up with notions when the boys ran out of their own. Once she took on a batch—six men, one right after the other—with the five who weren't involved standing by watching while the sixth made love to her. She forced each of them to make love to her in a different manner.

She would do anything.

Anything at all . . .

Except for one thing:

She wouldn't speak to Joe Gunsway.

It was strange, she thought. Joe was the only really decent guy she knew, the only one who didn't try to make her or anything of the sort. Even after the way she had treated him he still called her every once in a while, still seemed to be working to straighten her out.

And, for that reason, she wouldn't so much as speak to him. Whenever he called she hung up the phone as soon as she found out that it was him.

One time he caught up with her on the walk in front of her dormitory. She had just gotten through one of the bad moments and her head was spinning from the alcohol that was making its way through her bloodstream. He gripped her arm and she couldn't shake him loose.

"I want to talk with you," he said.

"What's the matter?"

"I just want to talk to you."

She tried to shake loose but he wouldn't let go of her.

"I'm busy."

"I don't care."

Suddenly she was angry. "What's the matter?" she demanded. "You mad because you haven't had a chance to lay me?"

He didn't say anything but his lips curled into a frown.

"Don't worry," she said drunkenly. "You'll get your chance."

"I don't want my chance."

"No? What's wrong—don't you think I'm a good lay?"

"I don't care whether you are or not."

"Then what's the matter?"

"I love you," he said. "That's what's the matter."

Chapter 9

She got rid of Joe. It wasn't easy, but a combination of ridicule and sarcasm finally managed to convince him that whether he loved her or not, his love was not returned. He left her at last and she went off by herself, looking once more for a man.

And, of course, she found her man for the evening. They went off together and did the usual thing in the usual way, with the usual results.

Then she went home.

It was a long time before she could fall asleep. She sat in her room and thought about Joe, thought that the only person who cared for her was a person she couldn't stand the sight of any more. Now he had told her that he loved her, and it wasn't hard to see that he was being serious about it.

He couldn't love her, she told herself. For one thing, she wasn't worth it. For another, he didn't know her well enough to know what he was in love with. He was in love with an image, a shadow without form or substance, and whatever love he thought he had for her existed more in his mind than in reality.

Still, his confession disturbed her. She didn't want anyone to love her, least of all Joe Gunsway. Wasn't it bad enough that she was ruining her own life? Did she have to louse him up too?

She went to bed about four that morning and lay there in the darkness listening to the sound of Ruth's measured breathing and wishing that she could sleep too. But she couldn't—she could only think the same thoughts over and over and wish the same useless wishes again and again.

There were two main wishes. Wish One was that she had never bumped into Don Gibbs, that she had kept leading the straight-and-normal life of a straight-and-normal coed, dating Joe two or three times a week, working in her courses, staying a virgin until she could be sure that the loss of her virginity wouldn't drive her to the sort of state she was in now.

Wish Two was different—Wish Two was that she and Don had been able to stay together, to love each other forever, to get married finally, to have children and live in a little house somewhere as a family.

Both wishes had the chance of a snowball in hell, she thought. Of a virgin in a den full of dedicated satyrs.

Which wasn't much of a chance at all.

When sunlight started streaming in through the window she gave up trying to sleep. She got out of bed and dressed, jumping a little when Ruth's alarm clock went off while she was getting dressed. She left the room before her roommate's eyes were completely open and went to the cafeteria for breakfast.

She took a tray from the pile and walked along, filling her tray with a glass of orange juice, a stack of pancakes, a few slices of bacon and a bowl of what passed for oatmeal. She paid the cashier and carried her tray to an empty table off to the side. The caf was practically deserted at that hour—it was too early even for most of the people with eight o'clocks—and she had a chance to be by herself. She was glad, too; she didn't think she would be able to take it if somebody tried to make conversation. Not the way she felt.

The gin she had had the previous night hadn't done the job for her. No sooner had she gotten rid of her depression when Joe Gunsway had deposited a bomb in her lap in the form of a declaration of love, and that neatly negated the effects of the gin. The sex hadn't helped either, and she was now more depressed than when she had started—tired but unable to sleep, starved but unable to eat.

She tried to eat but it didn't work. The pancakes were rubbery and she was afraid she would break the fork trying to cut them. The oatmeal was a soggy mess that was impossible to look at, let alone eat. The orange juice was bitter and she only managed to get half of it down. The bacon that morning was a Clifton Cafeteria specialty—half-burnt, the other half raw. Both halves, needless to say, proved equally inedible and unappetizing.

She sat at the table for almost three hours, her food untouched after the first unsuccessful attempt, a cigarette clutched periodically between her fingers and stubbed out in the ashtray when it had burned down to a butt. She didn't have anything to do or any place to go.

She still didn't feel much in the mood for sleep. But she realized that the combination of no sleep and no food had exhausted her enough so that she would pass out readily enough. She took her dishes and piled them on the tray, then carried the tray to the conveyor belt that would carry them back to the kitchen. She left the cafeteria, walking back to her dorm in a stupor, not answering the people who talked to her as she walked. Back in her empty room she collapsed on the bed fully clothed and slept.

She slept for twelve straight hours. At ten that night she opened her eyes and sat up. She was instantly awake, her eyes unclouded and her mind alert.

She felt worse than before she went to bed.

Her mouth, to begin with, tasted like a sewer. She had slept in her clothes and they felt as though they had been lived in for at least three months. Her arms and legs ached dully from the awkward position in which she had slept and her stomach was protesting audibly at the fact that it was nearly empty.

But this was nothing compared to the way she felt inside. The sleep, instead of curing her depression, had made everything just a little bit worse. She sat up on the edge of her bed and stared across the room at Ruth, who was reading a book. She sat there, her eyes studying the back of Ruth's neck, and she felt like reaching for the razor blade.

Instead she reached for the bottle.

The bottle was two-thirds full of gin. The first swallow was properly medicinal in flavor and properly alcoholic in content and she felt better the instant the liquid reached her stomach. She was tilting the bottle to her lips for another jolt when Ruth turned around in her chair, her lips parted slightly and her brow wrinkled into a disapproving frown.

"Linda—"

She took the second swallow.

"Linda, I wish you wouldn't start drinking like that. Honey, I'm awfully worried about you."

"Don't worry," she said.

"Linda—"

"Don't worry," she repeated. "I know what I'm doing."

"Do you?"

She nodded.

"Honey, you're killing yourself. You're letting one little fling with a smooth bastard named Don Gibbs turn you into a living corpse."

"More than one fling. He was only the first, Ruth. There have been plenty of others since then."

"Honey, they don't matter. None of this would matter if you'd only buck up. And for goodness sake put down that bottle—do you want to turn into an alcoholic?"

Linda put the bottle down on the floor. She stared at it for a minute, then picked it up again.

"Yes," she said thoughtfully. "There are a lot worse things to do than to turn into an alcoholic."

"Linda—"

"The life of an alcoholic," she continued with remarkable logic, "is not so bad a life. It is not nearly as bad as people make it seem. An alcoholic has one problem and one problem only. The problem is alcohol."

"Linda—"

"When an alcoholic has enough alcohol," she went on, "his problem is solved for the time being. When he wakes up he needs more alcohol, and once again he solves his problem. It's very simple, you see. He has a problem and he solves it and everything's fine and dandy."

Ruth shook her head sadly. She stood up from her chair and closed the book she had been reading. The book was Sepsonwol's *Fundamentals of Contemporary Economic Theories* and it didn't take any remarkable display of will power on Ruth's part to close the book.

She walked over to Linda and sat down beside her on the edge of the bed. Linda turned to look at her, thinking how petite and lovely the little dark-haired girl was and wondering why she didn't have the same type of problems. The answer, she guessed, was a simple one. Ruth may have lost her virginity earlier than Linda, but she was a good enough person so that an act like that wouldn't knock her for a loop.

"Honey," Ruth was saying, "you've got to get a grip on yourself. Isn't there anything I can do for you?"

Linda shrugged.

"Anything at all?"

She shook her head.

"Linda, why don't you go over to the psych department one of these afternoons? There are therapists supplied by the school that you could talk things over with—that helps a lot of people."

"What good would that do?"

"It might help you. Honey, you're not in so deep that you can't pull yourself out once you get straightened out inside. If you let one of the therapists have a few good sessions with you, you'd probably feel a lot better, if nothing else. How about it?"

"No."

"No?"

"No."

"Why not?"

"I don't want to."

"Linda—"

"I don't want to," she repeated. "I don't want any psychiatrist trying to take me apart and figure out what's wrong with me. I just don't care, Ruth."

Ruth didn't say anything this time, and Linda thought that it didn't matter what she did or where she went or who she talked to. Just so long as there was either a man or a gin bottle handy everything would be all right.

"Linda—"

"What is it?"

"Honey, this is silly, but I can't help feeling partially responsible."

"Don't be silly."

"I mean it—if I had been a better roommate maybe you wouldn't have taken everything so hard. Roommates are supposed to look out for each other, you know."

"You've been a wonderful roommate."

Ruth sighed, and Linda noticed that the shorter girl was on the point of tears. "Linda," she said, "isn't there *anything* I can do for you?"

Linda considered. She wanted to think of something if only so that Ruth wouldn't feel bad. "You could drink with me," she offered finally. "I'm going to drink this stuff anyway, and you could give me a hand with it."

Ruth forced a smile. "Sure," she said. "That way at least you won't be drinking alone. And it'll keep you from killing the bottle by yourself."

"Fine," Linda said.

And she tilted the bottle and took a long swallow. Then she handed it to Ruth.

"I don't know how you drink this stuff," Ruth said a while later. Linda noticed that her roommate was slurring her words slightly. Evidently the stuff was hitting her hard.

For that matter, Linda herself was getting hit pretty hard by the gin. It was landing on top of a very empty stomach, and the emptiness of her stomach seemed to balance against Ruth's lack of familiarity with gin. They were both about equally tight.

"It's not bad."

"But it tastes like medicine."

"I know—that's what I like about it."

"Oh," Ruth said. She took the bottle from Linda and took another long swallow. It didn't appear any more that she was drinking merely to keep Linda company. She took the bottle in her hand and drank long and deep, and there was a hint of desperation in her face as she drank the gin down.

"Ruth—"

"Whatcha want, Linda?"

"Rub my back, Ruth."

"Huh?"

"Rub my back," Linda was saying. "I think I'd like it if you would rub my back."

"I better not."

"Why not?"

Silence. Then: "I don't know. I just don't think I should, that's all."

"But why not? You're my good roommate, aren't you?"

"Uh-huh."

"Well, what's a roommate for?"

Ruth didn't say anything for a minute. Then she said: "Okay, Linda. I'll rub your back."

Linda kicked off her shoes and stretched out on the bed, waiting. Seconds later she felt Ruth's hands on the small of her back, working at the flesh there, relaxing the tired and strained muscles. Ruth was giving her an excellent massage, and the relaxation of her back muscles combined with the spinning of her head was very pleasant.

She sat up suddenly.

"What's the matter?"

"Be better with my sweater off," she said. She peeled off the sweater and unclasped the bra. Ruth was saying something, protesting, but Linda couldn't make out what the other girl was trying to say.

"Rub my back," she said.

Ruth did as she was told. Her soft fingertips prodded Linda's soft flesh and the effect they had was marvelous. Another sensation in addition to one of relaxation ran through the blonde girl's body but she didn't bother to analyze it.

She forgot everything—where she was, who she was, everything was forgotten. She felt as though she was floating in a sea of latex with an extra cushion beneath her breasts and two godlike hands rubbing her back.

"*God!*" someone said. Ruth, probably, she thought dreamily. But she didn't bother to think about it.

Then the two god-like hands were slipping lower and gripping her around the waist, lifting her. She turned sleepily and rolled onto her back.

Seconds later Ruth's arms locked around her body and Ruth's mouth came down upon her own mouth. She was too drunk to know what was happening, too deeply under the influence of the alcohol and the back massage to react at all other than on a purely sensual level.

No girl had ever kissed Linda before. It was a new experience unlike anything that had ever happened to her. Ruth's lips were soft, indescribably soft, and Ruth's tongue was sweeter than honey when it dipped between her own parted lips. Ruth's tongue caressed the inside of her mouth, touched her tongue and left it tingling.

The kiss was prolonged—slow and gentle and thorough. Linda's whole mouth was alive now in a wondrously new way and a soft but insistent fire was burning in her loins. She closed her eyes and stretched luxuriously on the bed.

Ruth broke away from her then. Linda was unsure what was happening but she didn't care. All she knew was that she wanted it to continue.

A second or two later it continued. This time when Ruth's body pressed down upon hers, skin as soft and smooth as Linda's was pressed tightly against her, breasts as lovely and perfect were touching her own bare breasts, and the soft sweet mouth was kissing her own mouth again. Automatically her arms wound around Ruth's body and pressed the girl still closer. She gripped the girl around the waist and let her hands trail down to cup Ruth's small hard buttocks.

Ruth was naked from head to toe.

Ruth released her again a moment later and Linda wanted to cry out. Then she felt Ruth's hands on her breasts, cupping them so gently and tenderly, fingering the two nipples until they were as hard as red diamonds. Ruth pressed her lips to the valley between the two breasts and her tongue flicked out and touched the soft skin there briefly.

Ruth kissed each breast in turn. Her mouth and tongue were always gentle even when they were most demanding, always loving even when they were most insistent. Linda felt herself being lifted and floated higher and higher. There was no urgency in the way she felt, no irresistible passion that threatened to explode any minute. Instead she drifted in the soft flood of physical sensation, calm and relaxed, her whole body receptive to Ruth's caresses.

She was only dimly aware of fingers that unzipped her skirt and pulled it down over her knees, only half-conscious of the same fingers hooking themselves under the elastic band of her black panties and drawing them over her hips and off. But she could not help being aware of those fingers when they stroked and kneaded the flesh at the tops of her thighs.

Ruth's caresses grew bolder until they were completely unrestrained. Ruth's fingers and lips and tongue coaxed her to a height of sexual excitement that was almost too much to live through and that was simultaneously warm and gentle and free from worry. Linda began to pant and her heart beat faster and faster.

Finally she tangled her fingers in the girl's short black hair and held Ruth's head in place, her own eyes tightly shut, her breath coming in short gasps, her muscles tense now and beads of sweat dotting her forehead.

The two of them lay there, Ruth giving and Linda receiving, both of them writhing and twisting in a mad embrace like drug addicts taking a cold turkey cure. Their passion rose to impossible heights till they arrived together at the peak of sensual pleasure.

Then, after the final moment of ecstasy had come and gone, they were both suddenly and completely sober, both suddenly and completely aware of just what had happened.

They parted at once. Each girl was overwhelmingly conscious of her own nakedness and it seemed imperative to conceal that nakedness before anything else. Linda grabbed up her skirt and sweater and put them on, not bothering with under-clothing for the time being. Ruth did the same—then, dressed again, they turned and looked at each other. Linda's expression was one of puzzlement and lack of comprehension; Ruth's eyes were clouded with shame.

"I can't . . . can't say how sorry I am," she blurted out. "I didn't want it to happen, Linda. You must realize that. If I hadn't had so damned much of that gin—"

"I . . . don't understand, Ruth. How did it happen?"

"I made love to you, Linda."

"Yes, I know."

"I . . . I—"

Ruth broke off. Her shoulders were trembling and she looked

as though she might burst into tears at any moment. Automatically Linda reached out a hand to touch her, to comfort her. Then, realizing that a touch of any sort had a different significance after what had passed between them, she let her hand drop to her lap.

"I'm a lesbian," Ruth managed to say.

Silence.

"Believe me," she said. "Believe me, I didn't plan this. I didn't want anything like this to happen ever. I thought we could be... well, friends... without anything like this happening. But I was drunk and you were drunk and I guess we didn't know what we were doing."

Linda didn't know what to say.

"You didn't know I was a lesbian, did you?"

She shook her head.

"I've been a lesbian since my second year in high school," she said. There was a note of something in her voice, half defiance and half pride. "Sheila Ashley and I have been making love together all year long."

"I see," she said. But she didn't see, not entirely.

"Don't you hate me?"

"Of course not."

"You must despise me—"

"Why should I?"

"Because of what I am."

Linda smiled vacantly. "I'm not in much of a position to despise anybody."

"But—"

"You couldn't help it," she went on. "Why would I hold it against you? It's not as if it was something that'll happen again."

"No," Ruth promised. "It's something that will never be repeated."

Linda learned quite a few things from Ruth that night, things she had never suspected and never would have suspected if the two of them had not wound up making love together. She found out that her roommate's sophistication and polish was more a cover-up than anything else. Ruth was tremendously frightened that her lesbianism would come to the surface. As it was, Linda and Sheila Ashley were the only two persons on the Clifton campus who had any idea of it.

As a result, she had to be very careful to act "normal." Actually she had made love with a boy once, but she was hardly as experienced with men as she had led Linda to suspect. The single attempt had been an experiment—and a failure. Ruth was homosexual and that was all there was to it.

Afterward, as she thought it all over, the most amazing thing about it all was that Ruth was so well adjusted to what she was. On the surface it seemed as though she had much more against her than Linda did, but Ruth kept up-to-date in her schoolwork, led an active life and made friends easily. She didn't drink, didn't get depressed and was generally happy and at ease.

Linda, the "normal" one, was a wreck. It didn't make much sense, she thought. And at the same time it occurred to her that there might still be a chance for her to make the best of it. Maybe, if she tried, she could make an adjustment the way Ruth had.

It seemed impossible. There were only six weeks left in the

school year, hardly time enough to get caught up. She was almost certain to flunk out at the end of the term.

But she could make a try. She could start going to classes, stop going to bed with men. Passing courses and staying out of parked cars seemed equally impossible on the surface, but she knew that it was the only chance she had for a livable life.

Chapter 10

She was walking along the path from the Science Building to the Union, thinking how beautiful spring weather could be when the sun was out and the trees were green and the grass was green too and the sky was blue with white puffy clouds blowing around in it, when Jim Patterson took hold of her arm. She stopped suddenly and one of the books almost slipped out from under her arm but she caught hold of it.

"Hi," he said. He flashed her a smile.

She smiled back.

"Busy, Linda?"

She nodded.

"Got time to go for a walk?"

At least, she thought, he was decent enough to call it a walk instead of calling a spade a spade and a piece a piece.

"No," she said. "I'm pretty busy, Jim."

"How about later tonight?"

"I'm afraid not."

His smile faded. "Okay," he said. "I'll see you."

"Jim—"

He turned and looked at her.

"Jim, I've reformed," she said, making it sound light. "I've turned over a new leaf, sort of. No more... walks. I'm too busy trying to stay afloat in my courses."

The smile returned to his face. It was a warm smile and she knew that he meant it when he said: "I'm glad to hear that, Linda. Good luck—I hope you make it."

He turned and walked off. She watched him go for a second or two, remembering the first time with him on his blanket on the golf course, remembering the other times since then that the two of them had been together. Then she started off toward the Union once more for dinner.

You're doing fine, she told herself as she hurried through a fairly tasteless dinner. *God alone knows if you stand a chance of making it, but you're putting up a good fight. You're doing your best, for whatever it's worth.*

And she *was* doing her best; that was the funny part of it. Ever since she and Ruth had made love in their mutual drunken stupor she had thrown herself into the scholarship game with the same zeal she had previously devoted to learning the finer points of the fine art of bedmanship.

Since that night she had not cut a class or failed to complete an assignment. It was embarrassing, going to a class where the professor didn't even recall her name, but she forced herself to adjust to the routine. She went to every class and after the day's classes were over she hit the books with a vengeance. She had to do more than keep up with the new material—she also had to work her way through all the stuff that she had missed so far in the course of the year. The first semester's courses were a lost cause, already failed, but she felt that she still had some semblance of a chance with the courses for the second semester.

But it was such a slim chance. She had to work every afternoon and evening until well after midnight, and all of Saturday and Sunday were also devoted to the arduous process of catching up.

Strangely enough, studying was turning out to be fun in its own weird way. For one thing, she didn't have to go the route alone. Ruth was always around—she was gunning for a straight-A average and putting in plenty of time at her books. With the two of them in the room, both studying to beat the band, it wasn't quite so lonesome a task as it might well have been otherwise.

More important, studying was beginning to provide the same sort of escape that drink and sex had given her before. When she buried herself in a book she could forget Don, forget the way she had acted and reacted, forget everything but the material she was trying to commit to memory. And in one respect it was a good deal better than drink or sex as an escape. She didn't feel guilty after spending an evening with a book, the way she had when her evening's companion had been a bottle or a boy.

After three weeks of studying like that she was fairly certain that she would be able to pass her exams if there were six weeks remaining in the term instead of three. As it stood it was a toss-up. But she had a chance, slim though it might be, and she wasn't ready to give up.

It was hard to get back into the rhythm of studying, especially in that she had never learned the rhythm properly to begin with. She did everything as systematically as she possibly could, inventing little helps for herself, making list after list and schedule after schedule, working her way down each list and sticking to each schedule as well as she could without killing herself.

Every morning the alarm rang at a quarter after seven; every morning she was out of bed the minute it rang. She would wash and brush her teeth and dress as if she were on her way to a fire. Then she would be off to the caf for a fast breakfast and two or three cups of coffee to get her mind in working shape.

When she had an hour or more between classes she spent it at the library. She managed to be doing something academic almost every minute of the day, and once she started one particular assignment she didn't stop until she had finished it. This was tough when the assignment in question was too far over her head, but after the first week and a half she was generally able to understand what was happening in each of her classes and to get by.

As she finished the second cup of after-dinner coffee she thought about that meeting with Jim Patterson on the way to the caf. It hadn't been the first time somebody had asked her, politely or more directly, to spread her legs and oblige him. But she had stuck to her guns so far and the propositions were steadily fewer and farther between. While she would probably never completely live down the reputation she had built up with such zest, at least not while she remained at Clifton, it wasn't as much of a handicap as she had thought it was. She would make it—if she kept working hard enough.

After dinner, after the tray was on the conveyor belt and the food being attacked by the various enzymes that attacked food, she headed back to her room. There was plenty of work on the agenda for that night—a book to be read, a paper to be written, a Spanish quiz to be prepared for. She climbed the stairs and hurried to her room, anxious to get going, anxious to bury herself in her work and get as much done as possible.

Ruth was there, seated at her desk with a book open before her.

"There was a letter for you," she said. "In your intramural mailbox. I picked it up for you."

"Where is it?"

"I put it on your desk."

She walked over to her desk and found the letter on top of her blotter. It was in a white envelope with the college letterhead and crest in the upper left-hand corner. She tore open the envelope, wondering what it was all about, and took out the letter.

She read it through once.

Then she read it through a second time.

Then a third time.

Then she said *Ruth!* in a small stricken voice and handed the sheet of paper to her roommate. Then, unable to stand any more, she fell headlong on her bed. She did not cry; she could not have cried if she had wanted to. Nor did she say anything more. She merely lay on the bed, unable to breathe, unable to think, unable to feel anything but the overwhelming shock of the letter.

Ruth took the letter from her and sat down with it. This is what it said:

Dear Miss Shepard:

I regret that it is my duty to inform you that, at a recent meeting of the Student Personnel Committee, it was the committee's decision that you be requested to withdraw for the coming year. Withdrawal rather than expulsion will keep your record clean, as it were, and will facilitate your continuing at another college if you should choose to do so.

If it is your decision to withdraw from Clifton, I hope you'll let me know within the next several days. If you should wish to discuss any aspects of the decision of the committee with me I will be available in my office Monday through Friday from 8:30 to 5 for the duration of the term.

Samuel Maples
Dean of Students

That was all.

"Linda—"

"Not now, Ruth. I have to get this book read in time for class tomorrow, and I have to grind out a paper and then there's a good fifty words of Spanish vocabulary that—"

"*Linda!*"

"—I have to memorize. And after that—"

"Linda, please!"

She closed her eyes and stopped talking, still lying face down on the bed, still numb and still unable to understand fully what had just happened to her.

"Linda, you can go and talk to him. When he finds out what you've been doing for the past three weeks, when he tells the committee that you're working now and that you're going to get through your courses—"

"It's no use, Ruth."

There was a dead note of finality in her voice.

"You've got to talk to him, honey."

She sat up on the edge of the bed, her face composed now and perfectly calm. "I'll talk to him," she said dully. "But it's not going to work. I can tell. He's going to tell me that it's just no use, as it were, and that he wishes me the best possible luck in whatever field of endeavor I eventually choose, as it were, and if I'm ever passing through the town of Clifton between 8:30 and 5 Monday through Friday—"

"The old bastard!"

"It's not his fault. I just got this new-leaf project a few months too late, that's all." She hauled herself to her feet, her face set, her eyes determined.

"What are you going to do now?"

"I told you," she said levelly. "I have a book to read and a paper to write and a good fifty words of Spanish to learn. I might as well get to work on them now."

Dean Maples was in his office the following afternoon.

Dean Maples was sympathetic.

Dean Maples was understanding.

Dean Maples was sorry.

"I'm very sorry," he said. "I'd like very much to tell you that there was a possibility that the committee might reconsider your case, but I'm afraid it's impossible. As you know, you failed to pass a single course in the entire first term. Since then we've learned from your professors that your attendance has been sporadic to say the least and that you're expected to fail again."

"But I'm going to pass those courses," she explained. "I've been working for three weeks now, Dr. Maples. And I'm sure I'll pass."

"It doesn't seem very likely."

"Give me a chance—if I don't pass them all I'll withdraw. Isn't that fair?"

He puffed at his pipe and looked long and thoughtfully at the inkstand in one corner of his desk. Then, his eyes still fixed on the inkstand, he said: "It's not just your grades, Miss Shepard. There are reports of your personal conduct that... uh... that influenced our decision."

As it were, she thought.

"That's changed, too."

Dean Maples closed his eyes for a moment. Then he opened them but kept them turned toward the inkstand. It was a fairly common-looking inkstand and Linda couldn't understand what was so fascinating about it. She wondered if the old man was afraid he'd blush if he looked her full in the face.

"I'm terribly sorry," he said. "I'm afraid the situation is impossible, Miss Shepard. I'd recommend that you consider transferring elsewhere, or plan to spend a year out of school with the option of reapplying to Clifton after a year's leave. Quite a few students have done that and have profited by it."

"I see," she said. She didn't see especially but the dean had paused for breath and she felt that she had to say something.

But now there was nothing much more to say.

"I'm going to pass those courses," she told him. "You don't believe me, but I'm going to pass those courses. Even if I can't come back."

"Well," he said. "I certainly hope you do, but—"

"Not so that I can transfer," she finished. "Not so that I can come back here."

"Why then?" he asked, temporarily derailed.

"If you have to ask," she said gently, "you'll never know."

She kept working, knowing that she would have to withdraw at the end of the term anyway, knowing that the work she was doing wouldn't keep her in school and wouldn't really do much of anything for her. But she had to prove to herself that she could do it, had to keep her head above water and wind up with her courses passed. Proving her point to Dean Maples was secondary; proving it to herself meant a lot more to her for the time being.

Besides, as it turned out it was easier to keep going than to stop. It was like the line in *Macbeth* about being so far steeped in blood that to go on is easier than to return. She was in the study habit now for better or for worse. It was normal to go to classes, normal to read and write, normal to spend all her waking hours at her desk. Learning was becoming an end in itself, strangely enough, and she was actually beginning to enjoy the whole thing.

It was ironic, she thought. Now that there was no more opportunity for her to go on with her work, now she was getting a kick out of it. If only she had approached the whole problem that way from the beginning! She was just starting to realize how different the whole thing might have been. If she had worked on her schoolwork while she was with Don, if a secondary interest in the academic part of school had kept her busy when she wasn't with him, then she might have had a chance to keep him. If she hadn't been so damned possessive because he was all she had, then he might not have been quite so anxious to get her off his neck. Well, whatever had happened had happened. There was no sense crying over spilled milk... or over a fractured maidenhead, for that matter.

Read and study and sleep.

Sleep and study and eat.

Eat and read and sleep.

That was about all she did, right up to the week of exams, right up to the last and hardest week of the term.

Just read and study and eat.

And sleep with Joe Gunsway.

It started one afternoon when Joe gave her a ring on the phone. It seemed he had learned what she was doing and wanted to give her a hand if she ever needed any help with anything. Of course there was nothing that she needed from him. She knew this and she knew that he knew it as well. It was just his way of saying that he was there, still in love with her, still ready to help her in any way he could, still anxious to be with her and to love her.

Her first reaction was one of revulsion. Why couldn't the dope just leave her alone? Didn't he know when he wasn't wanted?

Then the feeling changed. He was, certainly, a nice guy. As nice a guy as she had ever known. And he liked her as a person, and he wanted to see her.

Why shouldn't she see him?

She picked a time when she could afford a break for an hour or two. It was early evening—she could get her studying done after he brought her back, and her mind would be probably keener and more alert if she took a two-hour breathing spell first.

Once she had made up her mind to see him it was not hard to

get the ball rolling. She managed to bump into him "accidentally" in the caf that evening. They talked; she suggested that they go for a ride for a little while. She didn't have to push him into it—he was anxious to see her and glad that she wanted to see him.

When they were in the car she didn't tell him to park and he didn't consciously seek out a lover's lane type of situation. His car was getting fairly low on gas and he felt more like talking than driving, and it wasn't long before the car was parked in a relatively private spot on a relatively lonely road. Because the sky was still light and because neither of them had planned on anything of the sort, it didn't seem like a necking situation.

She found herself talking to Joe, talking easily and readily. She told him everything—from her arrival at Clifton right up to the present. He listened to most of it without saying a word, and just having him to talk to made everything a lot easier for her.

Thinking back on it, she couldn't tell what made him decide to kiss her or what made her let him kiss her. It just happened. One moment they were sitting together in the front seat of the car and the next moment she was nestled in his arms with her mouth to his. It was a gentle kiss, not sexual at all, but one kiss led to another and one thing led to another and . . .

The funny thing, she thought afterwards, was that she didn't really want him sexually and he certainly wasn't trying to seduce her. If anything it was the other way around. He kept wanting to stop, to avoid taking advantage of her, but she wouldn't let him stop.

The experience itself was neither the passionate love she had enjoyed with Don or the frantic sex she had experienced with all of the others. It was, instead, more an act of friendship than anything else. She knew that he wanted her, wanted her perhaps more than he wanted anything else in the world. She knew also that he would never have her because she would never love him. Giving herself to him was a small way of thanking him for his love without returning it.

They made love in the back seat of his car. While she couldn't say for certain, she was fairly sure that he hadn't had much experience in the past. He was awkward and unsure of himself, but the warm feelings she had for him more than made up for any slight incompetence on his part.

They made love quickly and when it was over she felt neither frustrated nor satisfied. She was somewhere in the middle between the two extremes, not guilty over what she had just finished doing and not entirely pleased with herself either.

Naturally it served to make him love her more than ever. But, after they had gotten dressed again and had returned to the front seat of the car, she could tell that he knew where he stood now, that some element of his love for her had undergone a metamorphosis of one sort or another. He would not be calling her on the phone now any more; he would not be grabbing her arm or chasing her around campus. Nor would he spend his time pining away for her in some dark room. Eventually, when he met a girl who was right for him, he would be able to forget her and concentrate on the new girl.

That was the way she wanted it.

It was the way both of them wanted it.

• • •

As he drove back to campus, one hand on the wheel and the other draped over the back of the seat, she sat close to him without touching him. And she felt close to him, too. She knew that he was as good a person as she was ever likely to know, and she realized that knowing him had done her a lot of good.

"Linda—"

She waited.

"I'm glad that it happened tonight."

She didn't say anything. The statement didn't seem to require an answer.

"But I'm a little worried that it might have been bad for you. That you might take it the wrong way."

"What do you mean?"

He couldn't go on, and after a minute she understood what he was getting at. He was concerned for her, concerned that the act of intercourse might cause her to slide back down to the state she'd just finished crawling back out of. Could that happen to her now?

No, she told herself. Not in a million years. Giving herself tonight had been a thoroughly different sort of thing, a healthy act as opposed to the sick and twisted sort of thing she had been in the habit of doing. If anything, making love with Joe would help her, help her to be honest with herself and decent with others.

"Don't worry," she said.

"I don't mean to—"

"I know. It's all right."

And everything *was* going to be all right. She was sure of it now, as sure as she could be of anything. All she had to do was keep going the way she was headed and she didn't have a thing to worry about. That was all—just keep plugging in school, keep going to bed early and getting up early, keep going to classes and studying hard and keeping her mind on what she was supposed to be doing. The rest of the world would take care of itself if she could manage the difficult business of holding up her own end.

He let her out at her door and she walked up the stairway to her room. She got to work at once, settling down at her desk with a book open in front of her. She scanned page after page, her eyes taking in a paragraph at a clip as she read through the book.

Next year would be a problem, she thought. Her parents would have to find out and in all probability she would have to strike out on her own. But somewhere she would find a college that she could work her way through, and from there on in everything would be all right.

Exam week came. The Spanish final was first and she walked into the exam room feeling confident and walked out of it feeling still more confident. It was amazing how quickly she had managed to get the language down pat once she had really started to work on it.

The English final was the next day and she was a little worried about it.

But before it was time to take the exam she got the shock of her life and all thoughts of tests and classes left her head immediately.

Chapter 11

There was no single act or event that brought the full force of the shock home to her. The shock came instead as a sudden awareness of something she should have known all the while.

This didn't make it any less of a shock.

She was sitting in her room, the Spanish exam over and done with, the English exam due the next day. She was at her desk, studying valiantly, when she decided to take a ten-minute break to rest her eyes. So she left her desk and sat down on the edge of her bed and let her mind wander.

She realized with something of a start that she was a good three days late for her period. This didn't shake her up too badly, since she had been late before without being pregnant. She digested the thought carefully and her mind almost managed to swing from that topic to another less dangerous topic when another realization came to her and her fingers began to tremble uncontrollably.

She hadn't had her period last month.

God in heaven, how could she have missed without being aware of it? It seemed impossible, but she was so caught up in the new routine of studying and living the good life that she had passed from one day to the next without even thinking about the whole thing. That meant that instead of being three days late she was a month and three days late, which in turn seemed to indicate—

That I'm pregnant, she thought.

She stood up and began pacing the floor of the room, up and down and back and forth. Her mind was reeling and she had trouble staying on her feet.

It was ironic, she thought. Now that she had managed to stop sleeping around, now that except for Joe she hadn't let a guy get near her in weeks, now she found out that she was pregnant. She might just as well have been sleeping around all along, for all it mattered to her now, for all the good virtue was going to do for her. But no—she had stayed pure as the driven snow. And now she was knocked up.

She had to be sure. One way or the other she had to know for certain, though she couldn't figure out how she could possibly be anything other than pregnant. She was rarely late and she had never missed completely in her life; the odds against a miss now were tremendous. It might have been different if she had been worrying lately about missing, because she knew that girls who were worried over pregnancy frequently missed a period for purely psychological reasons. But she hadn't given it a thought in the longest time.

How could she know for certain? There wasn't a doctor in town that she could go to. She knew there was a test that they sold in drugstores that you could take on your own, but the thought of picking one up in a Clifton drugstore was appalling. It would be all over town in a minute.

But not knowing was even worse. She decided quickly that she could grab a bus to Springfield where no one knew her and buy a pregnancy test at one of the drugstores there. Then she could take the test in a gas station rest room or some place and find out once and for all.

Maybe she wasn't pregnant. Maybe she was really all right and she just skipped for some reason she couldn't figure out. Maybe—

Well, she had to find out.

She closed the book on her desk, slipped on a corduroy jacket and hurried out of the dormitory. She raced down the stairs to the ground, along the path to the street, down the street to the main road of the town. At a lunch counter in town she bought a round-trip ticket to Springfield; then she waited outside for the hourly bus. She chain-smoked while she waited for the bus to come, lighting one cigarette from the stub of the last, her mind racing and her lips praying silently that everything would be all right, that she was not pregnant.

The bus came.

She sat near the driver and watched through the front window as the bus rolled along down the two-lane highway. The bus seemed to be crawling and she wanted to shout to the driver, to urge him to hurry and get her to Springfield so that she could find out what was the matter with her.

Finally the bus pulled into the terminal. She jumped up from her seat and got out of the bus, hurrying out of the terminal and rushing through downtown Springfield, not sure quite where she was going but knowing that she ought to be able to locate a drugstore somewhere in the general area of the bus terminal.

She found a drugstore after almost walking right past it. There was a male pharmacist on duty, a tired looking man with a green eye-shade and a soiled white shirt. He looked at her and his eyes were bold as he stared at the front of her blouse visible through the corduroy jacket. She wanted to button the jacket up so that the dirty little man couldn't look at her, wanted to run out of the drugstore and find some other place. But she forced herself to be calm, and her voice was normal when she spoke.

"I'd like one of those home pregnancy tests," she said.

The druggist smiled. She wanted to hit him, to wipe the grimy smile off his face.

"For your mother?" The irony in his voice was not concealed.

"No," she said.

"For whom?"

She didn't answer.

The druggist came out from behind the counter. She saw now that he was a short little man barely as tall as she herself was, a thin man with stooped shoulders. She guessed that he was about forty-five years old.

"Those tests are kind of expensive," the druggist said. "Run you close to five bucks!"

"I can afford it."

"Might not have to," he said. "I might be willing to give you the test free if you want."

His eyes eliminated any possible doubt as to what he was talking about.

He continued to ogle her and she continued to get quietly sick to her stomach. Was that what she was—a roundheeled tramp who would sell herself to save paying for a pregnancy test? Could the little weasel actually believe she would take him seriously?

"Just sell me the test," she snapped.

"No reason for you to be spending all that money!"

He reached out a hand and she watched, paralyzed and unable to move. His hand slipped inside her jacket and fastened on one of her breasts.

The hand tightened.

She kicked up, suddenly, automatically. She caught the druggist right where she wanted to catch him, right where it would hurt the most. An agonized moan sprang from his lips and he sank to his knees, holding himself where she had kicked him as if the touch of his hands would alleviate the terrible pain.

He was trying to say something but she didn't stay around to hear it. She turned and ran from the store, continuing blindly down the street on the run. After a few blocks she found another drugstore where the proprietor didn't leer at her and she bought the test.

The directions were simple enough. Instead of going to a gas station she took an inexpensive room at a second-rate hotel where she would be sure of complete privacy and ample time.

Before she took the test she stretched out on the sagging bed and closed her eyes. The test had to turn out negative, she told herself. She couldn't be pregnant—why, she wouldn't even be able to tell who the father was! It could be anyone of a dozen or two dozen boys.

She got up finally and took the test.

It was positive.

She was pregnant.

Naturally she didn't believe the test. She left the hotel and looked through the yellow pages of the Springfield phone book for a local doctor. She found one who was open and went to him for an examination.

The examination left no trace of doubt in her mind. The test might have been wrong but the doctor was certain.

She was pregnant.

By the time she reached the Clifton campus she wasn't sure how she had managed to get back. She couldn't remember anything that happened after she had left the doctor's office. She was in a daze all that time, walking without knowing where she was going, winding up at last at the bus station and getting on the bus for Clifton. She couldn't even remember the bus ride, couldn't remember getting off in Clifton and walking back to her dorm again. It was as if she had suddenly been transported from the doctor's office to her own room, as if she had teleported from place to place like a character in a science fiction story.

She was back in her room again, back in her room and quietly pregnant. The doctor had told her that she was almost two months pregnant, that the baby would be around in less than eight months. She got undressed now and stood in front of her mirror, wondering how long it would be before the new life that was growing in her womb began to show. Not too long, she decided. Not too long and her stomach would swell up and stick out, and anybody who saw her walking along the street would know what she had done and what had happened to her.

What would she do? Where would she go? She couldn't go home to Cleveland even if she wanted to, not the way she was now. And she remembered the verse to *Careless Love*:

What oh what will mother say,
What oh what will mother say
What oh what will mother say
When I come home in the family way . . .

Mother, she thought solemnly, would not be likely to approve. Any school that she might want to transfer to would be even less likely to cast an approving eye on her swollen stomach, for that matter. She found herself wondering insanely if any of the college catalogues had special information on the qualifications necessary for unmarried and pregnant applicants for admission. Probably not, she decided.

What could she do?

Two months ago she might have committed suicide and would at least have given the idea serious consideration. Now she rejected it the instant it occurred to her. Suicide wasn't the answer, not now, not when she was just starting to learn how to live life. Now there were too many things she was enjoying and too many things she wanted to do. She wanted to live, not to die.

Pregnant.

Well, she thought, this was one worry Ruth would never have. When two girls made love neither of them got pregnant. She prodded her stomach with her fingers, wanting to rip the fetus out of her womb and strangle it with her bare hands, and she almost envied Ruth at that moment.

What could she do?

Well, she could have the child—that was one answer. She could go off to some city where no one knew her and get a job doing something or other. God alone knew what kind of job she could get, but one way or another she would be able to get by. Nobody starved in the United States any more, and she could work up until the fifth or sixth month, maybe longer if she got the right kind of loose clothing to hide her condition from the world.

And then she would have the baby and go right back to work again. It wouldn't be much of a life, taking care of a kid and working, but lots of other girls managed to stay alive that way.

For that matter, she thought, she could give the baby away. She could have it and then give it to a couple who could provide a better home for it than she could. But after she carried the baby for nine months she might not want to give it up. Then where would she be?

Up the creek, she answered herself.
Up the creek in a lead canoe.
Without a paddle.

When the answer came it seemed too easy. She forced herself to do nothing at first and went back to studying for the English exam. But the page did somersaults in front of her eyes and she couldn't get any more studying done for the time being.

She left the dorm. At the cafeteria she had a tasteless dinner that she could only eat half of. Then she walked out of the caf and circled around the campus for around fifteen minutes.

Until she ran into Joe.

They met and they began talking. It was always easy for her to relax in a conversation with Joe and this was no exception. He wasn't going anywhere in particular and she told him that she wasn't either, so they wound up sitting on a bench in the middle of the campus, sitting side by side and talking easily.

The conversation roamed from topic to topic but she was careful never to get talking about what was really on her mind. It had seemed so easy when she had thought of it—tell Joe she was pregnant and he would offer to marry her. It was as simple as that.

She didn't love him. But he loved her and he would love her more if she met him halfway. He was the kind of guy who would marry her if she said the word, marry her just to keep her from having an illegitimate child.

That was the way he was.

And, she told herself, it wouldn't be such a bad deal for him. She would love him if she lived with him and she would make him a good wife—faithful and considerate, interested in his work and happy to be with him.

It made sense on paper.

But, as she sat next to him on the bench, she realized that she couldn't go through with it. Figuring out how logical it was didn't help at all when the chips were down. How could she possibly ask Joe to marry her? How could she possibly dare to cheat him out of the chance of real love, for a wife who married him because she loved him and for no other reason?

And, as she thought about it, it occurred to her that Joe wasn't the only one who would be cheated by that kind of marriage.

She would be cheated as well.

Oh, it would be convenient for the time being. But she would be stuck for life with a man she didn't love, a man who was marrying her out of the goodness of his heart and not because the two of them would be right for each other. And she would spend the rest of her life wondering what might have happened if she had had the guts to work things out for herself instead of jumping at the easy answer.

She didn't know what to do. But she did know what she couldn't do. She couldn't trap a guy like Joe, couldn't stick him with a marriage that didn't have a chance of working out properly. Joe was the kind of guy who could love somebody else's child as his own, but this didn't mean that he didn't have the right to a better life than that.

No, Joe deserved better and so did she.

She didn't tell him she was pregnant.

The conversation dragged on, finally dying by itself. Joe walked off in one direction and she walked off in another. The parting was more significant to her than just the end of a conversation. In a sense, Joe Gunsway was walking out of her life and she was walking out of his. There were only a few more days left in the period and they probably wouldn't see much of each other with exams and all. Next year he would come back to Clifton and she would be somewhere else.

But it was better that way.

She went back to her room. Ruth was there studying and Linda had a strong impulse to tell her, to share the horrible secret with the girl who had become her best friend in the world. Four times she was on the verge of blurting out the news and each time she changed her mind.

She didn't want to tell Ruth, she realized. She didn't want anybody in the world to know, not now and not later. She didn't want to have the baby, for that matter. She wanted to fall down a flight of stairs and have a happy little miscarriage. Or to go horseback riding and bounce the little bastard into the next county.

There had to be some way. She wasn't cut out to be a mother. God, she wasn't nineteen yet! What kind of a home could she give to a child?

But what could she do?

She sat down at her desk again. Studying had proven to be a better escape than sex or drinking—and, as it turned out, an infinitely safer one. Besides, pregnant or not pregnant, she was going to take that English exam tomorrow. She might as well try to pass it.

Once again studying proved to be a successful escape. She got lost in the book, lost in a world where Linda Shepard didn't exist and where all the women in the book seemed to be bereft of ovaries for all the thinking they did about sex and for all the sexing they did. In this respect the book wasn't true to life by contemporary standards, but at the moment Linda didn't mind this in the least.

She studied from 7:30 to 10:15. By that time the print was doing a little dance on the page and she decided that she deserved a rest for a while. She closed the book and took a walk outside.

It was a warm, clear night. The stars were out and the moon was full enough so that she could see where she was going without any trouble.

She walked aimlessly at first but after the time spent studying her head was a good deal clearer and she didn't feel as bad as she had felt earlier. Now she was able to concentrate on the problem at hand and to get some idea of the possible solutions she had.

She didn't make much headway at first. Then she got an idea—there was one person in the world who could help her, one person in the world who would know exactly what to do.

One person.

Chapter 12

The phone rang three times before he answered it. Then she heard him lift it from the hook and say: "*Hello.*"

She took a deep breath.

"This is Linda," she said. "Linda Shepard."

He didn't say anything and for a moment she was afraid he was going to hang up on her. She listened to the silence, her fingers trembling once again, her throat tight.

"I have to see you," she said desperately.

"What for?"

"I don't want to say over the phone."

"Don't worry," he said. "The line's not tapped."

"This one might be."

He laughed at that. "C'mon over," he said.

Then there was the sound as he replaced the receiver. She didn't hang up right away, however. For a long moment she stood with the receiver next to her ear and listened to the silence, hardly able to believe what she had heard, hardly able to believe that Donald Gibbs had just gotten through telling her that it was all right for her to come over to his apartment. Then, hardly aware of what she was doing, she hung up the phone and drifted down the staircase and out the door.

•   •   •

He was waiting for her and the first thing she thought was that he looked the same as ever. His hair was still cropped close to his head and his beard was neat and well-trimmed. His eyes looked impossibly tired and there were deep lines in his forehead and around the corners of his mouth. She wondered how long it had been since he had had some sleep; the combination of the *Record* and final exams must have been keeping him awake constantly.

"Come on inside," he said. He led the way and sat down on the edge of his bed; she took a seat in a chair across the room from him. He didn't say anything and she didn't know just where to begin.

"Okay," he said finally. "Let's have it."

She still didn't know what to say. Her nerves were on edge both from what she had to talk to him about and from the experience of seeing him again, of being with him at his apartment. She had passed him in halls during the past few months and had run into him in the cafeteria from time to time but they hadn't spoken before, not since they broke up.

"You're so tense you're shaking," he told her. "You better let me have it."

Abruptly she said: "I'm going to have a baby."

Nothing registered in his face. He didn't seem particularly surprised or shocked or upset.

He said. "Whose?"

"I don't know."

"How long have you known?"

"I just found out today."

"When's the happy day?"

"I'm about two months gone. Maybe a little more."

He nodded. He pulled a pack of cigarettes from his shirt pocket and lit one for himself, offering the pack to her more or less as an afterthought. She took one and lit it herself, dragging deeply on it.

"What do you want from me?"

"I don't know."

He stared at her thoughtfully. "You must want something," he said. "We haven't spoken to each other in months. What is it that you want?"

In a small voice she said: "Help."

She couldn't look at him now. She turned away and looked at the wall instead, then puffed nervously on the cigarette. She tried to blow smoke rings but the smoke refused to form circles and trailed to the ceiling in shapeless wisps.

"Linda—"

She turned to him.

"Do you want to find a guy and get him to marry you?"

She shook her head.

"Sure?"

"I don't want to marry anybody."

"Then what *do* you want?"

Help, she started to say again. Instead she said nothing and started to turn away from him once more. Maybe it was a mistake coming to see him, maybe he couldn't help her at all. She didn't know what to do or what to say.

"I'd heard you reformed," he said lightly. "I heard you stopped trying to set local bedroom records."

She nodded dully.

"How come?"

She shrugged.

"Are you coming back here next year?"

She shook her head.

"Why not?"

"They threw me out."

"Grades?"

"Partly."

"What else?"

She tried to smile but it didn't work. "Local bedroom records," she said.

"Oh."

"I'm going to pass my courses," she offered. "I've been studying day and night and I'm going to pass everything. I told the dean that but he said it didn't matter."

"Dean Maples?"

She nodded.

"He's a son of a bitch."

She nodded again, thinking that she ought to say something but not having anything to say.

"What are you going to do next year?"

"I don't know."

"Going home to Cleveland?"

"No."

"Transferring somewhere else?"

"I'd like to," she said. "If there was some place where they would take me. I don't think there is."

"If you pass your courses—"

"That doesn't matter," she said. "That's secondary. First I'd have to find a college that admits unwed mothers, and that knocks out a lot of them."

"Oh."

She put her cigarette out in an ashtray. She didn't stub it out viciously but ground it out gently, methodically. She wasn't as nervous as she had been now; somehow talking to him was very relaxing. Just the fact that someone else knew was a help, and Don wasn't scolding her or condemning her or berating her for her condition. He was listening to her, questioning her and, indirectly, helping her.

She felt a little better already.

"Linda—"

She looked up.

"Are you positive that—"

She told him about the test and the examination.

"Who knows that you're pregnant?"

"The doctor," she said. "But he doesn't even know who I am and he wouldn't care if he did."

"Nobody else?"

"You—that's all."

He closed his eyes for a minute or two, thinking. Then he opened them and stared fixedly at her for several seconds.

"Linda," he said levelly, "you are not going to have that baby."

He stood up, walked to the telephone and sat down in a chair next to it. He put the receiver to his ear and dialed the operator.

"New York," he said.

When the New York operator was on the line he said: "Person-to-person to Mr. William Norment, ORegon 4-0527."

He waited while the call was placed.

"Bill?" he said after a moment. "This is Don Gibbs... okay, thanks. Look, Bill—I don't want to talk much. I want to ask you for a name and number."

Silence.

"The name is that of one of your benefactors," he said. "As I understand it, he's a fairly big operator."

He smiled then and began writing something on a pad next to the phone. "Swell," he said when he had finished. "Give my love to everybody, fellow."

He hung up the phone.

"You're not going to have that baby," he told Linda. "Bill's an old buddy of mine. When a girl he knew got into some difficulty due to the spontaneous failure of a piece of rubber goods, Bill had to do something about it. Rather, he had to find somebody who would do something about it. I just got the name and number of the somebody."

She didn't understand.

"This guy," he said, indicating the name on the pad, "is possibly the only really reliable rabbit-snatcher in the western world. Outside of Sweden, that is. In Sweden this sort of thing is all open and aboveboard, but here in this middle-age country of ours—"

"Rabbit-snatcher?"

"One of the more picturesque American colloquialisms," he explained. "It means abortionist."

"Abortionist?"

"Linda," he said, "you're going to have an abortion."

She looked blank.

"You're not going to have that baby, and next to a kick in the stomach the most logical way not to have a baby is to have an abortion. Isn't that what you wanted when you came here?"

She thought for a moment. "I don't know," she said honestly. "I didn't think of it that way. Somehow an abortion never even occurred to me. I just thought you'd be able to do something to help me."

He didn't say anything.

"Don, isn't it dangerous?"

He shook his head.

"You hear lots of stories—"

"Sure," he said. "You can go to one of these old women who cut you open with a filthy butcher knife. But this guy is reliable."

"Are you sure?"

"Positive. He's a human contradiction in terms—a dedicated abortionist. He does the job because he believes certain people have a right not to have babies and certain babies are better off unborn. Take a case like yours—what chance would a kid have with nineteen-year-old unmarried mother? He's got two strikes against him the minute he's born, not to mention the way it ruins your life."

She nodded, agreeing with him.

"This guy's a regular doctor," he went on. "A Pittsburgh surgeon with a large legitimate practice. Abortions are a sideline and he does them for very little money right in his own operating room. He doesn't try to make a profit on it—he's not that kind of guy. I don't think he even makes expenses on the abortion part of his business."

"But isn't it illegal?"

"Of course."

"Then—"

"Hell, he doesn't advertise. If the cops know about him they also have the good sense to leave him alone. And the medical association takes care of its own—they're not going to give him a hard time. It's not as if he was taking risks. If a patient's healthy and in the early months of pregnancy an abortion's less risky than an appendectomy—a good deal less risky."

"I see."

"I've got his phone number right here," he went on. "I'll give him a ring in a few days and you can fly down and have everything taken care of. A few days bed rest afterwards and you'll be as good as new."

She nodded.

Then she said: "Don, I don't know how I'll be able to afford it. Even if he's inexpensive and all there's the plane trip and the time in bed and—"

"I'll take care of it."

She started to say something but he interrupted her. "I've got the money," he told her. "I'm okay financially right now and I won't miss the dough."

She didn't know exactly what to say. All she could think of was how he knew exactly what to do. One conversation with her, one phone call, and everything was going to be all right again. She couldn't believe it, and she wanted to be able to say something, something to sum up the way she felt about it all.

She said: "Why?"

He looked at her, puzzled.

"Why are you doing this, Don? Why are you doing all of this for me?"

He smiled. "I'm just philanthropic—that's all."

"I mean it."

He looked away. "I suppose I feel partly responsible," he said.

"That's silly—it's not your baby."

"That's not what I mean and you know it."

"I know. But you shouldn't feel responsible anyway. What happened was my fault. I was too young and too mixed up to know where I was and by the time I got straightened out it was almost too late."

"And now?"

"Now I think I'm all right. I've been living clean lately, Don. It's like I'm not the same person I was a few weeks ago."

"You're not. You've changed a lot, Linda Shepard from Cleveland."

She smiled.

"I'm not even too sorry about what happened," she said. "I learned from it. I grew a lot older—sometimes I feel almost... well, ancient."

"I know what you mean."

"I wish—"

He waited.

"I wish I had known what I know now when I came here. I suppose that sounds like a line from something, but it's true in this case."

He nodded.

It was hard for her but she said: "I wish I had known all this when I... met you. I think things would have turned out a lot differently. I would have known how to... to love you."

He didn't say anything.

"I messed things up," she said.

"It wasn't all your fault."

"If I hadn't tried to smother you—"

"We were too different," he said. "You clutched at me because you were afraid I was going to run away. I ran away because you clutched at me. And because I was afraid—"

"Afraid?"

"Afraid I wasn't going to get away. Afraid I was going to care too much about you."

She was puzzled. "What do you mean? You weren't in love with me, were you?"

"Of course I was."

She didn't know what to say.

He saved her by changing the subject. "Any idea where you want to go to college next year?"

"I'm not sure. Where are you going?"

"I'm going to grad school. I figure I'll go to New York and get a job of some sort."

"On a newspaper?"

He shook his head. "I've had a bellyful of newspaper work with the *Record*. I think I'll try to get my foot in the door either in advertising or public relations. They're supposed to be looking for bright young men."

"Like you?"

"Not like me—but maybe I can fake them out."

"How about your girl?"

"*What* girl?"

"Aren't you going with anybody?"

"No."

Before she could say anything he added: "I haven't gone with anybody since you."

Again she didn't know what to say.

"I didn't want any other girl," he went on. "I thought I did. I thought all I wanted was to get rid of you."

He lit another cigarette, offering the pack to her. She didn't want one.

"I messed things up with you," he said. "We had something pretty good going and we were both too dumb to realize what was happening. All we did was louse each other up."

She knew suddenly that she was going to cry. There was a lump in her throat and her eyes were starting to cloud over. She thought how silly it was to cry over a love that was dead and buried, and then she began to realize that it was not dead and not buried, that she loved Don more than ever, that she had never stopped loving him, that she probably never would stop loving him. She clenched her teeth to keep from crying but she knew that the tears were going to come.

He spoke with difficulty. "I kept trying to hurt you," he said. "I'm beginning to realize why. You were the first girl I ever really loved, Linda. The only one. You had me scared silly. The only way to get out from under was to hurt you, and—"

Then she was crying. She got up from her chair and half-stumbled, half-fell across the room and into his arms. His arms went around her and he held her as she cried, her eyes overflowing with tears and her whole body shaking with the sobbing. He held her and stroked her and for a long time neither of them could say a word.

Finally she was able to get up. She sat beside him on the bed and he took her hand in his. They didn't look at each other.

"It would be very hard," he said.

That was all he said but she knew what he meant.

"Terribly hard," he continued. "It's not easy to pick up the pieces and put them back together again. It's harder than starting from scratch."

"I know."

He turned and looked at her. "I think it's worth a try," he said.

"So do I."

"I can't let you go now, Linda. I'm only beginning to realize how much I love you. I'm not going to let anything spoil it, not now."

She couldn't speak.

"Do you love me, Linda?"

"You know I do."

"And I love you. I never told you that before, did I? I was afraid to say it. Maybe I didn't even know it at the time—maybe that was part of it. But now I'll say it. I love you, Linda."

He put one hand under her chin and brought her face close to his. His lips touched hers and he kissed her.

"I love you," he said.

"Oh Don—"

He kissed her again.

"I don't know exactly what's going to happen, Linda. But there are a few things that I do know. We're both going to finish up here. You're going to pass those exams of yours and I'm going to graduate and get that silly diploma they hand out to you after you've finished wasting the prescribed four years here.

"Then we're going to pile into the car and drive to Pittsburgh. If the car gets that far—I don't know if it will or not. Then you're going to have your abortion and we're going to stay in Pittsburgh until you're well enough to travel.

"From Pittsburgh we're heading to New York. I'm going to find a place to live and then get a job. You're going to find a place to live—"

"The same place you find?"

He shook his head. "Not right away," he said. "That's got to wait until we're both ready for it. There are too many things we've got to learn first, Linda. And we're going to have loads of time—time to find out more about each other. Time to love each other."

He was right.

"Then we'll find you a college," he went on. "You ought to be able to get into NYU without a hell of a lot of trouble. A year there and you'll be a New York resident and you can go tuition free to CCNY. It's a free school and it's a hundred times better than this hole."

He closed his eyes, then opened them again. "God only knows what's going to happen after that. Maybe we'll find out that we hate each other. Maybe we'll quietly drift apart and never see each other again. Maybe what we've got will just disappear.

"There's another possibility. Maybe we'll find out that what we've got is worth keeping—worth keeping forever. It's too early to even think about that yet, Linda. But it might happen."

She nodded, not trusting herself to speak.

"We won't make the same mistakes again."

"No," she said, "we won't."

She looked at him, loving him, needing him. But she loved

him and needed him in a different way now. She wasn't afraid of him or afraid of losing him, not now. She felt safe and sure of herself and sure of him. For a moment she felt terrible about all the other boys she had been with since that first time with him, but then she told herself that they didn't matter, that they never really existed. They were a child's substitute for the real thing. Now she had the real thing, and at the same time she was no longer a child, no longer the girl who had first come to Clifton.

He reached for her and drew her close to him. His finger touched her cheek and ran down her face to her chin. He kissed her lightly on the lips, then kissed her closed eyes and the tip of her nose.

He took a deep breath and held it. "I want you," he said. "Christ, I want you more than I've ever wanted anything. But we're going to wait for a while, anyhow."

"Okay."

He smiled. "Besides," he added, "with a woman in your condition—"

He laughed when she started to blush. "You better go now," he said. "You've got to lick that exam tomorrow and I've got one of my own to worry about. We'll have plenty of time later."

She stood up. "Plenty of time," she said.

He kissed her once more. Then she left.

The walk back to her dorm was easy. She started studying immediately, sure of herself, sure that the exam would be no problem at all for her. There would be problems coming up, plenty of problems, but now she knew that she could handle anything that came her way.

She was a big girl now.

She wondered idly what it would all be like. NYU, CCNY, New York City, the whole thing.

She wondered what it would be like to be Mrs. Donald Gibbs.

Well, she would find out. She would learn all the answers and find out all that had to be found out.

There was plenty of time now, she thought.

Time for everything.

My Newsletter: I get out an email newsletter at unpredictable intervals, but rarely more often than every other week. I'll be happy to add you to the distribution list. A blank email to lawbloc@gmail.com with "newsletter" in the subject line will get you on the list, and a click of the "Unsubscribe" link will get you off it, should you ultimately decide you're happier without it.

Lawrence Block has been writing award-winning mystery and suspense fiction for half a century. You can read his thoughts about crime fiction and crime writers in *The Crime of Our Lives*, where this MWA Grand Master tells it straight. His most recent novels are *The Girl With the Deep Blue Eyes*; *The Burglar Who Counted the Spoons*, featuring Bernie Rhodenbarr; *Hit Me,* featuring Keller; and *A Drop of the Hard Stuff,* featuring Matthew Scudder, played by Liam Neeson in the film *A Walk Among the Tombstones.* Several of his other books have been filmed, although not terribly well. He's well known for his books for writers, including the classic *Telling Lies for Fun &f Profit,* and *The Liar's Bible.* In addition to prose works, he has written episodic television (*Tilt!*) and the Wong Kar-wai film, *My Blueberry Nights.* He is a modest and humble fellow, although you would never guess as much from this biographical note.

Email: lawbloc@gmail.com
Twitter: @LawrenceBlock
Blog: LB's Blog
Facebook: lawrence.block
Website: lawrenceblock.com